BLAKE'S PROGRESS

BLAKE'S PROGRESS

Nigel Kemble-Clarkson

Copyright © 2022 Nigel Kemble-Clarkson

The moral right of the author has been asserted.

Apart from any fair dealing for the purposes of research or private study, or criticism or review, as permitted under the Copyright, Designs and Patents Act 1988, this publication may only be reproduced, stored or transmitted, in any form or by any means, with the prior permission in writing of the publishers, or in the case of reprographic reproduction in accordance with the terms of licences issued by the Copyright Licensing Agency. Enquiries concerning reproduction outside those terms should be sent to the publishers.

Matador
Unit E2 Airfield Business Park,
Harrison Road Market Harborough,
Leicestershire. LE16 7UL
Tel: 0116 2792299
Email: books@troubador.co.uk
Web: www.troubador.co.uk/matador
Twitter: @matadorbooks

ISBN 978 1803130 842

British Library Cataloguing in Publication Data.
A catalogue record for this book is available from the British Library.

Printed and bound in Great Britain by 4edge Limited
Typeset in 11pt Minion Pro by Troubador Publishing Ltd, Leicester, UK

Matador is an imprint of Troubador Publishing Ltd

To dearest Suzie, who believes in my novel abilities

ABOUT THE AUTHOR

Nigel Kemble-Clarkson was born in 1939, the only child of a City ship broker and a portrait painter.

Following a Sussex prep school education, initially during Hitler's 'doodle bugging', he attended Brighton College where sport was the focus of his achievements.

Nigel then thrived during an extended obligatory spell in the Army where he ultimately served with the Royal West African Frontier Force and witnessed Nigerian Independence in 1960.

On returning to civilian life, he became a Lloyd's marine broker, swiftly rising to executive level with extensive international travel duties and also becoming a founder member of the famous (Goldfinger) Posgate syndicate. In 1975 he set up a highly successful broking company with two colleagues.

Despite a turbulent romantic life, Nigel remains close to eleven children and stepchildren and, now retired, lives with his wife in Isleworth whilst being proud of having been the longest serving full-time broker in Lloyd's of London.

ONE

To his extreme irritation, Richard Blake had to admit to himself that Rose was really getting to him.

His initial involvement with her was yet again as a result of his inability to avoid capitalising on the fact that his fine physique, dark good looks and laid-back disposition made him a prime romantic target for the opposite sex.

Nevertheless, as he had only just got over ruining a good marriage via his irresponsible philandering and was in the process of fitting in with his first non-military career, now was not an opportune time to be embarking upon an intense loving involvement.

Although Richard was a generally gifted and intelligent man, his bizarre sense of humour and lack of self-discipline whilst serving with the Royal Fusiliers had let him down on more than one occasion.

With this in mind, his commanding officer, mentor and friend, Lieutenant-Colonel Bill Barnham had been brutally frank on meeting up with him shortly after his recent demobilisation.

"We are seriously missing our outrageous Captain Blake and life is certainly a great deal duller for everyone without your illuminating presence. However, even though I managed to get away with extending your nine-year commission three years ago, after your last personal scandal and dramatic divorce, I was under zero pressure from the hierarchy to persuade you to serve with us any longer. Let's face it, Dick, in spite of your inspirational leadership qualities and resilience in dire straits, our army is not as yet geared to your 'swinging sixties' style of behaviour. However, as we nudge into the seventies, I am certain that your new Lloyd's of London job will fit in far more appropriately with your social modus operandi."

What Bill then more seriously added rendered Richard somewhat taken aback.

"I should have encouraged you to join the City's Artist's Rifles but I felt that you were not a natural 'terrier'. In which case, if you do not permit the strength and fitness of your six-feet, two-inch frame to be degenerated by expense account excesses, with your 178 IQ, you might enjoy being involved in subtler patriotic duties."

The colonel had then handed Richard a card with a central London telephone number typed on it as he added, "I will ensure that these people are expecting to hear from you. Believe me, I consider that many of your undoubted skills may now be much in need as numerous situations are currently deteriorating around the world, not least of all just across the Irish Sea."

No end of badgering could then induce Barnham to

provide any further information concerning his somewhat insistent suggestions and observations.

Nonetheless, before Blake got around to making the mystery call, three days later he received papers through the post appointing him as a captain in Her Majesty's Officer Special Reserve Corps. However, on then immediately phoning the number that he had originally been given, an anonymous person merely abruptly instructed him to await further orders.

After a number of weeks had passed with no contact from this source, the matter paled to insignificance, during which time Richard found himself unsuccessfully grappling with romantic entanglement.

His relationship with Rose Gallagher of Killarney originally began with a remarkable lack of subtlety when, shortly after becoming a Member of Lloyd's and commencing his City career, he received a mysterious phone call in his office.

"Hi, Dick; well, it appears that my two mountains are now obliged to come to Mohamed. This is Rose and I hadn't realised that you were so plastered at Julia's bash last Thursday that you lost my phone number, which has to be why you have failed to call and invite me to the intimate dinner for two which you promised."

Richard had attended Julia Rosko's party in Markham Square the previous week but was certain that he had not chatted up anyone called Rose and rarely allowed alcohol to blur his sense of priorities.

Nonetheless, with an alluring female voice on the line there was only one possible response. "Rose, my dear lady, of course. I had to make a quick business trip to Norway and was about to phone you. How about seven-thirty tomorrow night at the Savoy American Bar. I shall reserve the only alcove which, as I am sure you are already aware, is just by the incoming stairway."

With immediate agreement and the threat of an identity problem minimised, phase one of the interloper's objective had now all but been achieved.

***

Rose's mission was clear, but a tad awkward as her London-based IRA controller, Liam Riley, happened to also be her regular boyfriend with whom she was sharing a cramped and seedy bedsit in Earl's Court.

Via intelligence easily gleaned from Irish infiltrators after the 1969 commencement of a new Provisional Irish Republican Army campaign, operatives within the UK's secret services were easily identified.

Sure enough, as she descended the celebrated hotel bar's stairs, there was her target. In contrast to her tatty photograph of him, and to her distinct relief, he appeared to be a well-groomed, ruggedly handsome young man who, complete with drink and cigarette, was lounging in the nearby alcove.

In similar vein, Richard Blake was more than pleasantly surprised as a sumptuous-looking young lady approached him, in spite of the fact that he was certain that he had never set eyes on her before. However, although this was an obvious set-up, with her piquant features and bodily curves undulating beneath a fashionable magenta silk caftan, he was instantly persuaded to go along with the masquerade.

As he stood up to greet her, she tossed her bobbed auburn locks and coquettishly scrutinised him with a pair of lustrous deep blue eyes.

"Rose, absolutely wonderful to see you again; all's well that ends well. What can I get you to drink?"

Having brushed lips with Richard and crossed her shapely booted legs as she settled into the alcove's sofa, she replied, "Great to see you too, Dick. You shouldn't play hard to get, naughty boy! I will drink some of what is making you look so fit."

As a hovering waiter hurried off to procure two large Jack Daniels on the rocks, her willing victim could not resist a quick tease. "Julia Rosko was looking radiant at her party the other night. Her modelling career is obviously still booming."

"Wow, I thought so too, and she really is an irritatingly gorgeous creature," was the reply.

Game, set and match! The lady in question was a wealthy journalist and as plain as a pikestaff, but what the hell!

"Well, Rose, I must ask you, is that charmingly subtle lilt in your accent American or Canadian?"

"Darling, the answer is neither. Even though I was at school in New York, as many of my family settled there during the last century following the potato famine ravages of your Duke of Wellington, I am proud to say that I am Emerald Isle through and through."

Having already won a non-showbiz 'darling', Richard nudged the boat out a little further. "In that case, as I am certain that you are an ardent Roman Catholic, we must endeavour to liven up your next confession a little."

Her gratifying response to this was a caressing knee squeeze, which, by the time they were into their third JD, had progressively advanced towards Richard's adventure zone.

On draining his glass, the old soldier then volunteered, "I believe that the time may now be ripe to employ some camouflage for your forward manoeuvres in the form of a Savoy Grill tablecloth and advance to phase two of our operation."

"I cannot begin to imagine what your battle plans for phase three might be," was his guest's encouraging reply.

During the inevitably delicious repast which ensued, it became clear that, in addition to her gratifying demeanour, twenty-three-year-old Rose possessed the quick wit and diverse personal input of a highly intelligent and well-read individual.

She also seemed flatteringly eager to quiz Richard over his military adventures and shared some spicy stories about her recent student experiences at Dublin's Trinity College, where she had secured a first in history.

All in all, the evening was a howling success and crying out for consummation by the time crepe suzettes were being devoured.

"So, Dick, that large green object that you have just concealed under your napkin looks remarkably like a room key attachment."

Putting down his fork, the not-too-guilty host caressed the lady's finely tapered, perfectly manicured hand.

ONE

"Call me an incurable romantic, but I love the Thames and fervently believe that post-prandial coffees and liquors are far more enjoyable if consumed in the privacy of a river-view suite."

Any resistance to Richard's lightly veiled suggestion was non-existent and matters were graphically enhanced when, on immediate arrival at the pre-planned destination, Rose urgently uttered, "To hell with your coffee and liquors; let's grab some champagne later."

With that, she instantly denuded her now writhing exquisite form and expertly assisted with Dick's more complex disrobement, before impatiently spread-eagling herself upon the ample king bed's counterpane, wearing only her boots.

***

On arriving late at his City office the following day, Richard Blake made a solemn oath that, in the interests of his new dedication to personal independence, the supreme perfection of the previous night must not be repeated at any cost!

This was notwithstanding the fact that, by lunchtime, the firm's now forewarned and forearmed telephone girls were being persistently pestered by an increasingly infuriated Irish lady.

Otherwise, Richard was highly relieved that, as he was still residing in temporary accommodation at Ebury Street's Eden Plaza Hotel, there was no identity exposure on the home front. Also, further pressure at the office was then obviated by an impromptu three-day Norwegian trip to establish whether or not some of his erstwhile military contacts in Voss may be commercially useful.

Meanwhile, the aspiring Lloyd's broker was blissfully unaware that, as the days went by, his rebuffed one-night stand's home front situation was dangerously deteriorating.

Although Liam Riley displayed all the charm and bonhomie of a regular Irish gadabout, he was fundamentally a foul-tempered vicious sadist. Ironically, he possessed about as much love and respect for humanity as Al Capone, the infamous hoodlum that Riley's stunted film star double, Rod Steiger, had recently depicted on screen so brilliantly.

His venomous nature eventually boiled over when he ran out of patience and assaulted Rose with a harsh back-handed slap across her face one morning. The impact of the blow was sufficient to propel her across their cramped kitchen where her head struck an antiquated grimy stove, which caused her nose to gush with blood as Liam grabbed the front of her dress.

"That should have been a proper right jab, except that I don't want to mar your pretty features too much just in case 'lover boy' condescends to get in touch with you after all. Christ almighty, it's been over a week now, you must have been a lousy shag."

Having long been accustomed to chauvinistic violence, there was no way that Rose O'Leary was going to accept this treatment lying down and, having grabbed a carving knife from the sink, she confronted her snarling, but now retreating, aggressor.

ONE

"Listen, you bastard, if I was a 'lousy shag' it is probably because I have been sorely out of practice recently. I can assure you that Mr Blake could teach you a thing or two and you still have not told me why it is so bloody important for me to hook up with him."

With considerable difficulty, Liam got a grip of himself and sat down at a tatty Formica-topped table. "Grab me a breakfast scotch and I will fill you in, but remember that if the powers that be, who are already sticking hot coals up my arse, find out that I've let the cat out of the bag, it could be curtains for both of us. I still have doubts over your true devotion to the cause, anyway."

Following Rose's silent pouring of two whiskeys before sitting down with him still nursing her blade, he continued, "As you know, the true Irish Army's offensive is now well into its second year and, although our hits are mainly confined to the scum in Northern Ireland, as we progress into the seventies, our war will increasingly focus upon the swine over here. This will include a destruction of key targets, where I have been tasked with City of London objectives, including the fucking Tower, believe it or not! You won't know this, but Lloyd's of London, where your secret service quarry happens to work, is this country's biggest invisible export and at the top of my hit list."

Having then grabbed the knife from a now slackened hand, he added, "So, you'd better think up something to sort out your cock-up as your next bollocking will not be from me and will likely be a lot more conclusive!"

TWO

RICHARD'S FIRST CIVILIAN CAREER HAD IN NO small part been inspired and promoted by one Toby Wellington-Green, who he had originally met at a Tower of London City Executive dinner when the Royal Fusiliers were performing garrison duties there some years before.

Toby was an archetypal Old Etonian who, with his charm, chiselled features and ever-immaculately clad, athletic frame, cut a dash with both sexes. He had also had a 'good war' as a gunnery officer, which included a spell performing the duties of Lieutenant-Colonel in Burma when he was but twenty-two years old.

Following a night on the town together after the Tower banquet, he and Richard had become firm friends and always endeavoured to meet up when circumstances permitted. During their get-togethers, female pursuit would often be on the agenda as Toby's Norwegian, ex-SAS air stewardess third wife was about as faithful to him as he was to her.

TWO

It had been at a lunch at the Ritz in 1969 that Toby had persuaded his young friend to seriously consider embarking on a Lloyd's career, in spite of considerable resistance.

"Please do not bring that up again as I have no wish to discuss the matter. Insurance is boring and I intend to be doing something a great deal more interesting with my life when the army lets me go shortly."

Toby's jaw had jutted forward determinedly as his steely blue eyes locked into his guest's rebellious gaze across the table. "Stop being so bloody pig-headed, Dick, and listen. Until the end of the last century, Lloyd's mainly covered ships and their cargos, and that side of the business is still lucrative, socially fascinating and full of opportunities for overseas travel in great style. Damn it, your estranged father has been a Baltic Exchange ship broker for years and lived the life of Riley. In addition to which, your mother received the rare honour of being invited to launch a Norwegian tanker a few years ago, for which she was generously rewarded.

I am now formally offering you a job in my company as a marine director/broker, where I am certain that you will be slavering over the remuneration and extravagant perks that such a position is worth."

As Toby relaxed into his seat, with an adjustment of his customary red carnation, a now half-convinced Richard Blake raised what appeared to be a reasonable question. "How about the fact that I possess no knowledge of insurance whatsoever?"

The reaction was swift and vehement. "Dick, you are a highly fluent gentleman with a keen brain, not an inarticulate bloody technocrat. I am the chief executive of a major Lloyd's broking firm and know fuck all about insurance. Nevertheless, I do employ many eager beavers that do who are ever on hand to brief me. They write the specific risk scripts and then, with the skill of an actor, I absorb the gist and embellish it with sufficient humorous panache to seduce the underwriters into contributing their capacity. Somewhat akin to our favourite pursuit: get 'em laughing and you are halfway to the bedroom! It really is as simple as that and, let's face it, old man, we both know that it doesn't really matter what you do to achieve your objective, so long as you never tell lies and do it with style!"

So, just over a year after this conversation, here ex-fusilier Richard Blake was, plying his new trade in the smart Lloyd's arena – which he regarded as Petticoat Lane with suits on – when he was summoned to the market caller's rostrum just before midday.

The 'waiter' then delivered what should have been, but in all truth was not, an unwelcome message.

"Young lady who needs to see you urgently at the main entrance. She didn't say why, sir, but apparently she is a bit of all right!"

The relatively novice marine broker, who was still attempting to become accustomed to the overfamiliarity of NCOs in 'civvy street', hurried to the main reception area where, on attempting to take Rose in his arms, he received a spirited slap around his face. Following this, just to make matters more humiliating, the top-hatted, red-robed door waiter loudly enquired, "Is this person bothering you, miss?"

TWO

To which the brazen beauty instantly replied, "Not at all; Mr Blake is about to show me round your famous Lloyd's exchange, and he had some shaving soap hanging off his ear."

To defer further inappropriate comment from the patronising senior lackey, Richard flashed his Lloyd's pass, which instantly deflated the man's pompous air of authority.

"I see, sir, and of course it is totally in order for you to conduct this lady around the Room as a Member Elect," was his response as he obsequiously cringed.

Before proceeding, Blake sat his intrusive minx down on a foyer sofa. "I am truly sorry for being so evasive, but our first encounter was just too idyllic, and a deep romantic involvement is not what I need when I am trying to build a new life. In fact, I must have suffered what the military might call 'a lack of immoral fibre', but I am now overjoyed to see you again, in spite of your spirited pugilistic skills.'"

Rose, who was looking radiant in a classic fuchsia two-piece suit and cream scarf with her shapely stockinged legs balanced on excessive gold stilettos, smiled thinly.

"Well, although that sounded like more than a modicum of bullshit, I have to admit to having sorely missed you and sincerely hope that you are now prepared to share a slice of your newfound independence with me. Now, let's take a look at what I always thought was the head office of Lloyd's Bank."

The two-floored layout of the 1958 Lloyd's Building that Rose was about to be shown was not dissimilar to Edward Lloyd's coffee house, where ships and cargos were insured three hundred years earlier.

The basic desks, known as 'boxes', at which underwriters offer cover capacity, evolved from former coffee stalls, whilst brokers, who might have originally doubled up as waiters, negotiate shares of coverage at the best price on 'slips', from which an insurance policy derives.

Until 1971, females were banned from these hallowed precincts unless accompanied by a male member. A restriction which naturally led to a great deal of rather pathetic schoolboyish behaviour from brokers and underwriters whenever a lady was escorted round the market. In his 1930's cartoon series depicting Lloyd's, Henry Mayo Bateman brilliantly captures this scenario in *A little ray of sunshine visits Lloyd's*.

The picture depicted a swanky young fellow parading his delectable girlfriend through the underwriting room whilst traders with elongated necks and popping eyes ogled her. Nothing much had changed!

Nonetheless, Richard's stunning, self-assured guest focused her interest upon artefacts such as the Lutine Bell, the traditional Loss Book record and letters from Emma Hamilton to Lord Nelson on display, rather than paying attention to childish leering.

She also conducted herself with the poise of a dignified film star during Richard's numerous personal introductions.

Nevertheless, en route to the Nelson Exhibition Room on the first floor, she did overdo things a tad by indulging in an Evita-style waving session from the balcony to the entire marine market below.

Notwithstanding this, the unplanned tour turned out

to be a delight and was embellished by a boisterous follow-up lunch in the ever-popular Short's Tavern, next door.

During its progression, many of Rose's new Lloyd's fans clamoured to join the couple's ample table and 'soldier boy's' popularity in the market received a mega boost.

However, as soon as the lunch bill was settled at 4.20pm, Richard's priorities came to the fore. With their carnal focus urgently stirring, the happy couple wasted no time in securing a west-bound cab, and as they rounded Hyde Park Corner, the specific final destination was revealed.

"Now then, Rose, I have just moved into a new apartment in Tedworth Square and, as it is a bit of a dump, I really need some refurbishing guidance from you."

The candid response was sceptical. "It certainly should not be that much of a dump as it is not far from Sloane Square. Anyway, having now managed to retrieve your attention, I should let you know that I am currently involved in a long-term relationship. It is in all truth a typical family-geared Gallic hook-up with little affection, but I do live with a man in an Earl's Court eighteen-carat dump."

Richard's non-committal response was. "I would be amazed if a lady with your many qualities and assets has ever been without a partner, but I trust that this one is not an over-possessive jealous type."

Any possible response was masked by an anticipatory kiss as the cabby came to a halt in Tedworth Square.

Having then entered the newly leased apartment, Rose's first comment was, "How could you possibly moan about this place? It's a bloody palace."

This was a more than fair comment as the maisonette's layout adhered to the latest open-plan design, with a spacious drawing/dining room, plus a downstairs loo and two bedrooms and a box room on the second floor, as well as lavish bathroom facilities.

His new interior design advisor's only further comment was, "Presumably the more than adequate furniture is included as part of the deal, but the walls could be livened up a bit with some decent pictures."

"Actually, my love, I have a few which are still in store and include some Wiley prints and a couple of Buttersworth square-rig oils."

The reply that Richard received from his nymph conveyed her obvious anticipation of his prime intent.

"I haven't got a clue what you are on about, but I would have thought that, with your obvious dosh, you could afford to buy some subtly obscene nude paintings. However, following that sumptuous boozy lunch, I feel that we have truly earned an immediate siesta and, although I adored wallowing in the wild passion of our first encounter, this time I am going to subject you to some military-type discipline. If you adhere to my strict programming, here and now, I shall eventually allow you to explore, caress, penetrate and possibly lightly abuse every mound, fold and orifice of my anatomy. For a start, kindly remove all your clothes immediately."

Starting with Rose's luscious lips, followed by her frequent urgent repositioning, several hours passed before their raw, aching and pungent slippery bodies collapsed in a satiated heap on the main bed.

TWO

Tragically, though, in spite of their joyous bonding session, with more to come, some dark, dangerous clouds were looming on the horizon for both of them.

***

On yet another tardy office arrival the following day, Richard was greeted with an urgent request from Daphne the receptionist to telephone a number which he identified as his OSR contact.

Having then complied and been requested to hold on, an affected, brittle male voice aggressively came on the line.

"Blake, is that you? Where the hell have you been and why have you left your hotel without advising us of a new home number? You are now a serving officer again so, having just read your file, bloody well behave like one for a change."

With a tender head and other parts of his anatomy, Richard was in no mood for this apparently unwarranted aggression.

"Listen, you guys have so far failed to provide me with any operational information concerning OSR since I was appointed almost four months ago, and I am not accustomed to being shouted at out of the blue. Who the fuck are you and what is your status?"

"McCarthy MC and I totally outrank you. It is vital that we have a face-to-face meeting as soon as possible, so you had better be available," was the staccato reply.

Somewhat taken aback by his unforeseen re-entry into military-style discourse, Captain Blake adopted a more civil form of address. "Sorry, sir, but I was rather shaken by this shot out of the blue. Of course, I am at your disposal, so let me know exactly where in the MI6 building your office is and I should be with you in about fifteen minutes."

Another 'clanger' had been dropped as the reply forcefully displayed. "How dare you make any top-secret organisational assumptions over the telephone, have you no sense of security? I am obviously aware of your appearance, so be at Jason's Espresso Bar, near to Embankment tube station, in twenty minutes' time. Make sure that you are not late."

The call ended.

McCarthy's demeanour unquestionably matched his mode of address so, having arrived first, Richard had no doubts over the identity of the bowler-hatted, pencil-moustachioed middle-aged athlete who strutted towards his table.

Then, with no handshake or offer of refreshment, the archetypal martinet aggressively launched into his topic the moment his rear-end contacted a cheap plywood chair.

"Colonel McCarthy. So, Blake, how come you were escorting a London-based IRA sub-agent around Lloyd's of London yesterday? You know perfectly well that now hostilities have recommenced, the building is highly likely to become a prime terrorist target. Not only do I find this incident incomprehensible, but also, as you have somehow managed to identify and root out this treasonable criminal, what is your excuse for failing to report your minor coup to the OSR, in which you are supposed to be a captain?"

TWO

As gimlet eyes bored into his, Blake found himself nearer being lost for words than he had been for a long time. Nonetheless, he did manage to remember that, when one is in a tight corner, always switch into an aggressive stance and lie through your teeth if necessary. In other words, pursue a course which the military refers to as 'initiative'.

"My answer is quite simple, sir, I do not make reports until I have acquired what I consider to be adequate useful data. As you most probably already know, many dedicated Irish nationals reside in Olympia who naturally frequent pubs in the vicinity. I met Miss O'Leary in one of the area's more extreme Gaelic taverns a couple of weeks ago when she was in company with numerous known agitators and decided that it would be fruitful to become acquainted with her…"

The colonel rudely cut in, but at least his crass remark divulged that he was most probably not aware of the Savoy encounter.

"With your disgraceful reputation, I am certain that 'fruitful' has a lustful interpretation!"

Secretly relieved, Captain Blake continued, "As you insist upon raising it, I have certainly had some intimate moments with this lady but have been somewhat hamstrung by the fact that she lives with some bloke in Earl's Court. The Lloyd's excursion was admittedly at her request, and I saw no harm in it as the only security aspects that she witnessed were a load of red-frocked retired servicemen wearing funny hats."

McCarthy pulled back his chair and stood up. "The 'bloke' in Earl's Court that you so casually mention is one Liam Riley, a senior Irish subversive operative whose speciality happens to be blowing up buildings, you bloody idiot! You will in future refer to me and address me as 'Falcon' and I want a full written report concerning your relationship with Rose Gallagher posted to me via registered mail by close of play today."

With that, the martial nightmare strode from the café, having slapped down a card on the plastic tabletop. On examining it, Richard was amused to note that the address given was in the same block as MI6 and his sense of the bizarre was tickled when, on turning the card over, 'Your code name is JINGLES, always use it in future' was scribbled on the back.

It was high time to move on from the humdrum café and find a gastric pub where he could sensibly review the imbroglio into which his life had just been plunged.

Following the quaffing of two negronis in the nearby Coal Hole, Richard came to the conclusion that the bottom line, although dead simple, was going to be incredibly tricky to handle.

In addition to him now being erroneously presumed by the hierarchy to have artfully pinpointed Rose, she was under IRA instruction to spy upon him and would have no idea that he had now been made aware of it.

Meanwhile, the formidable, all-powerful McCarthy was not someone that he would seek to mislead for fear of getting shot at the Tower of London!

The only rational conclusion was to play matters by ear and proceed with caution but, as Richard was to about to dramatically discover, the personal aspect of his situation would soon tragically deteriorate.

TWO

***

"What the hell are you blubbing about, Rose? You have been a right misery since you got mixed up with your Protestant bastard. I admit it was a clever move to lumber him in Lloyd's the week before last, but you have now stayed out all bloody night with him five more times since."

Even the heartless Liam was shocked by the reply he received from his mistress as she endeavoured to staunch her tears. "You were the one who urged me to get close to him but if you can't take the heat, I will happily get out of his kitchen, even though I imagine that for me to do so on your instructions will not delight our big shots.

Actually, if you really want to know, I am mourning another Protestant. My highly distraught mother phoned whilst you were out to tell me that Uncle Semus was blown to bits yesterday when that pointless Armagh bombing got screwed up. As you know, it was him who cared for me and helped bring me up when my father buggered off and, in spite of his choice of religion, I always adored him and will miss him enormously. Don't forget that not all your family are Catholics either."

Riley half-filled a tumbler with brandy. "Yes, and I would cheerfully shoot every one of the fuckers. Your 'darling' uncle was also in the RUC, for Christ's sake, so he deserved to die like all the rest of those snivelling bastards. Start behaving like a proper patriot for a change."

At this malicious retort from a man that she was now growing to hate, something inside Rose snapped and, having temporarily blinded him by chucking the brandy into his face, she grabbed an iron poker from the fire hearth and forcefully hit him over the head.

Then, whilst he was temporarily comatose, she bundled some clothing, cosmetics and toiletries into a large holdall and swiftly vacated the sleazy premises.

Unfortunately, in her panic to escape before Riley recovered, Rose failed to grab any cash so, with all the banks now closed, she was in dire need of sufficient funds to take a steamer from Holyhead to Ireland.

Her instant plan was to keep well away from Belfast and hide out with a maiden aunt in Cork, who had always doted upon her.

There was only one possible solution so, praying to God that Richard might have arrived home from the office by now, she hastily wended her way along the Kings Road to Tedworth Square. Then, as she was desperately banging on the door with her thumb pressing the 21a bell push, she almost had a heart attack as her neck was firmly gripped from behind.

"So, I had not realised how desperate you were becoming to see more of me!"

With relief surging through her at the sound of Richard's voice, she turned to give him a passionate embrace as he fumbled with his keys and let them both in.

"Actually, darling, your timing was bloody lucky, as I was just dropping off my briefcase before going for a piss-up with the boys in The Australian up the road. What gives with the baggage?"

TWO

Whilst sipping a large glass of Sauvignon Blanc, it did not take long for Rose to recount a cautious version of her dramatic day's happenings, which temporarily plunged her lover into an uncharacteristically pensive mode.

Then, having gulped down the dregs of his bourbon on the rocks, Dick gently took her hand.

"I am devastated to hear of your tragic loss, but do have no worries on the cash front as I can give you all that you need from a wedge that I was going to spend on a Georgian sideboard that I recently I spotted in the Antiquarius market. Nonetheless, I am not sure that it is a good idea for you to go rushing off to Ireland. In fact, I must say that in the unlikely event that you have not divulged this address to the horrid Liam Riley, in order to avoid his inevitably punitive reaction, it is most probably preferable for you to stay here whilst you weigh up your options."

Rose dropped Richard's hand as she sat back in shock. "I have never revealed my shit of a boyfriend's name to you. What causes you to think that he is so dangerous and why do you assume that I am likely to have given him your address? The only possible answer is that you are fully aware of the fact that I have been far from straight with you. Nonetheless, I swear by God that Liam is under the impression that our meetings take place at the Eden Plaza Hotel."

Dick put his arms around his enemy undercover agent and kissed her on the nose. "I trust that is so, for your sake, but listen to me for a moment, my sweetheart. I must confess to being aware of your calling and the fact that you pursued me because of mine. However, I sincerely hope that the tragic demise of your uncle goes some way to convince you how totally pointless indiscriminate slaughter is and what freakish monsters people like your hopefully now ex-boyfriend are."

Rose's final reaction to these revelations was poignantly emotional as her tears began to flow. "And I thought that you were genuinely fond of me."

Taking Rose in his arms and smiling into her beautiful eyes, Richard sympathetically levelled the score and added a bonus, "Hey, wait a minute, I could make a similar accusation, as we have both been guilty of dishonesty. Nevertheless, I happen to be on the verge of falling deeply in love with you."

"To hell with Holyhead and Cork for the time being," was her reply.

***

Captain Blake was convinced that via his tough boarding school experiences, plus twelve years' military service, the theory about bullies being pacified if one strikes back at them with greater aggression, was spot on. Thus, when reporting to his superior officer over the telephone next morning, he grabbed the initiative with no holds barred.

"Ah, good day, Colonel; Captain Blake here. Due to an unexpected development, I need to urgently meet up with you and make a report."

The reply was predictably dictatorial. "Right, we will RV in the as before location at 1145 hours and remember, Jingles, that you have been ordered to call me Falcon."

TWO

Richard gritted his teeth. "Not workable, sir. As I have an important Simpsons-in-the-Strand business lunch at 1300 hours, I will meet you in the Savoy's American Bar for cocktails on me at noon... Falcon."

With that, the new Jingles hung up his phone and left the office to grab a cab in order to ensure that he arrived at his destination with sufficient time to occupy the bar's only private alcove.

Having done so, he was musing upon his last encounter in the same comfortable niche, whilst sipping a Tio Pepe, when a less than happy Falcon stomped down the bar entrance's short stairway.

Surprisingly, though, his opening remark then gave an uplift to his subordinate's opinion of him. "You've got a bloody nerve, but as it is now your party, I require a large Manhattan and I am not that happy about the level of security in here."

"I would have thought that one is far less likely to encounter Gaelic low life in this august environment than in the down-market dump you appear to prefer."

The extra aggression was obviously working as the colonel actually smiled when his cocktail arrived.

"It is the 'high life' ones that are the most dangerous. So, Captain, what sudden amazing event are you so eager to share?"

After Richard had completed his subtly edited briefing, McCarthy sat back contemplatively and, having demanded a refill, came up with a totally inappropriate solution.

"Well, Jingles, as the girl obviously has to be confined to your home, which, I would hazard a guess, is unlikely to remain secure for long, I will send over one of my expert lady interrogators to debrief her."

Blake slapped the table. "Take it from me, sir, I now know Rose well and I am sure that she would not respond positively to any form of officialdom. I am afraid that you will have to leave the garnering of any useful information she may have to my tender persuasion."

The martinet took a gulp of his fresh drink.

"Well, Jingles, I am not going to override your superior and obviously intimate knowledge of the matter, but I normally only rely on my female agents to glean intelligence sexually. Who do you think you are, James Bond? Actually, apropos of my last remark, as matters are becoming somewhat more volatile, did you retain some form of hand firearm on leaving the army?"

"A Smith and Wesson 38, Falcon," was Richard's reply, which inspired a snort of derision from his superior, who immediately withdrew a package from his briefcase.

"Just as I thought. So, how are you going to discretely carry a cowboy cannon like that? Take this parcel, inside which you will discover a nine-millimetre calibre, nine-shot Beretta with plenty of ammunition, an appropriate armpit holster, plus, for more discrete occasions, an easily fitted silencer."

The remainder of Richard's brief session with Falcon during 'one more for the road' was almost bearable and, at times, even bordered upon being amusing!

THREE

Following his pleasantly excessive Simpson's lunch and a tedious late afternoon board meeting, Richard did not arrive back home until 7.45pm.

On then preparing to enter his apartment, he was irritated to observe that, although the landlords had embellished the entry portal in accordance with his wishes, some of the light oak varnish appeared to have stained the blue carpet at its base. Then, when he was attempting to push open the door with some difficulty, he perceived, much to his surprise, that the stain bore a distinctly red tinge.

It was at this point that horrific realisation took hold as Blake suddenly rushed to a nearby ashtray in the hall and stubbed out his cigarette with a shaking hand.

The smell of violent death is a gruesome, tangible odour which only those who have experienced it will recognise with horror and the ex-warrior was now certain that this dreaded phenomenon was clearly present.

On eventually forcing the door open, he discovered

that its obstruction was a severed shapely leg that had so recently encircled his loins.

His inadvertent macabre focus upon this remembrance automatically obliged him to resist the heaving pressure emanating from his gut. However, on entering the nearby loo, where a blood-frothed breast was floating in the hand basin, he was forced to violently vomit by the familiar, but now partly toothless and punctured, head which glowered at him from the lavatory bowl.

Having then become emotionally numbed by the revelation that his apartment was wrecked, blood-covered and adorned with the intestines and body parts of his late lover, Richard stumbled out across the square to seek some form of solace in the local Red Lion pub.

As he gulped down his third large scotch, the ageing barman remarked, "So, Dick, glad that you decided to finally settle 'ere now that you are out of the 'mob'. You ain't lookin' like your old self, though, is everythin' OK with the noo flat?"

Richard swallowed hard and just managed to utter, "A few problems with guests, that's all. I am going to use your public phone in the passageway."

He had just realised that, before alcohol addled his already devastated brain, he must report to Falcon which would now involve using the 'Only in Express Emergencies' number which was inscribed upon his controller's anonymous card.

Having identified himself as Jingles the moment the call was answered, he received a Falconry bark. "I trust that this is not from your home telephone as it may have already been tapped."

THREE

On confirming that he was ringing from a phone box, Richard hastily relayed his disastrous tale, ending with, "As 'Safer in Earl's Court' was scrawled in blood across the only pane of glass left in the French windows, there is little doubt who the perpetrator was."

The response was characteristically insensitive but succinct. "No need to be quite so phobic old fella. Getting emotionally involved is always inadvisable in our game and you must never forget that whatever happens, you are a soldier first.

I agree there is little doubt that Riley is the culprit and, when our call ends, I will ensure that Scotland Yard immediately raids the Earl's Court address that you have already given me. You are forbidden to perform any reactive exploits and as returning to your flat is obviously out of the question, I suggest that you check into your former hotel where I will endeavour to keep you posted."

Falcon then totally broke out of character. "In the meantime, I am sorry for your obvious grief. These things are sent to try us, but as stalwart troopers, I am afraid that sometimes we can do no more than think of England. I will ensure that the Tedworth Square debacle is promptly sorted out, with a discrete, respectful and godly interment of the corpse and full constructional and decorative renovations."

When the line then went dead, Blake immediately called the Eden Plaza to book himself a room before knocking back a final drink.

An hour and a half later, he received Falcon's promised update as he unsuccessfully toyed with a chicken sandwich. Apparently, Liam Riley was not in evidence at his home and the police had confirmed that there was every indication of his recent hurried departure.

Early in the morning two days later, the colonel called back to arrange another meeting, where this time his chosen location was a decent Covent Garden pub, the Kemble's Head.

Whilst swilling their first pint of bitter, Falcon explained that Riley had skipped the country and sought sanctuary with Noraid in Manhattan, an institution which provided Irish-American assistance and support for members of the IRA.

"In that case, sir, that is where I shall be in the very near future, as I have every intention of settling the score with that venomous, murdering animal," was Blake's impetuous, if tactless, reaction to his superior's update.

Naturally, the colonel did not concur with this passionate outpouring. Nonetheless, as he planned to draw Blake more deeply into his organisation and was ever keen to harm the IRA whenever possible, he decided to play his next card craftily.

"Listen, Jingles, if you insist upon enforcing recriminatory actions in New York, I may allow it, but only if you agree to cooperate with our agents on the ground. Also, be aware of the fact that, mainly for diplomatic reasons, if you fail to work with this team and get caught by the enemy, you will be totally disowned, not least of all by me. Our senior controller in Manhattan is Major Petula Larkin, code name 'Petal', so if you are determined to pursue your unwise vengeful mission, I shall put you in

THREE

touch with her. Also, you cannot be part of a USA operation without having a counterfeit alternative American identity with full papers and a bogus passport. This procedure, I would hasten to add, is to protect the service, not you. If you contact my ADC tomorrow morning, he will sort out everything that you will need in connection with your standby Yankee status."

As the stilted atmosphere during their second pint indicated that Falcon was still not too happy over Jingles' recriminatory intentions, the two of them soon went their separate ways.

***

The fact that Toby Wellington-Green's benignly relaxed image was a smokescreen to obscure his keen intelligence and powers of observation was largely what enabled him to orchestrate and firmly control a highly successful business.

Having been summoned to his office at 10.30am a couple of days after his Kemble's Head meeting, Richard Blake was invited to settle in a comfortable Louis Quatorze chair in front of his boss's expansive desk of the same ilk.

For most of the staff, this would be regarded as a cause for relief when complying with summonses from the governor, as to be kept standing was a sure sign that the invitee was considered to have erred in some way.

As Toby nimbly uncorked a bottle of Krug and filled two glasses, Richard once more admired the wall embellishments of his opulent bureau. These included a full set of Bateman's cartoons, depicting aspects of Lloyd's and fine oil paintings of naval engagements, such as Trafalgar and Abukir Bay.

Having then informally toasted one another, Wellington-Green came straight to the point. "So, Dick, what's with your sudden request for tickets and funds for a trip to New York? Surely, you can't have associated with any potential clients there during your military career?"

This question had been fully anticipated.

"Well, sir, I was involved in some Washington diplomatic duties a couple of years ago where I became very friendly with one Gilles Barton, a Louisiana Congressman. He has since been replaced at his own request earlier this year and now lives on Park Lane in Manhattan. Nevertheless, I am sure that he still maintains close links with his family in New Orleans who partly own and fully manage the locally based Mark Line Fleet of over fifty assorted vessels. I wish to get over there promptly as I am obviously keen to secure the fleet's insurance programme and, on phoning Gilles a couple of days ago, I learnt that he is shortly due to embark on a Holland-America world cruise with his wife."

All that Richard said was true, apart from the imminent holiday factor, and caused Toby to sit back with a relieved smile on his face.

"Well, Dick, that is bloody brilliant and, as your German and Scandinavian introductions seem to be starting to pay off already, you must obviously make the trip as soon as possible, with my blessing. My authorisation is given in spite of the fact that I am

THREE

prepared to lay a bet on your also sneaking in a call to crazy old New Orleans and probably Las Vegas as well! Nonetheless, whilst you are in New York, do make yourself known to our existing downtown clientele and try to milk them for some new enquiries. My secretary will give you their details.

Incidentally, permission for this venture is strictly subject to your residing in Fifth Avenue's Plaza Hotel, as it is the only hostelry in that fading city that retains a modicum of style. I might add, whilst we are grabbing an all-too-rare moment together, that without dreaming of asking you any leading questions, I suspect you are not completely free from serving Her Majesty as yet."

Following this typically perceptive observation, their entente switched into a more light-hearted mode, during which Toby promised Richard a long overdue night on the town when he returned from the States.

***

Having left a message on Major Larkin's answer machine announcing his arrival, Captain Blake was less than amused when his first vodka martini cocktail of the evening in the Plaza's Oak Bar was interrupted by a message announcing her response.

The pleasant-sounding female voice that coolly greeted him over a lobby telephone had a faint Californian twang. "Sorry for being unavailable earlier, I am now free and ready to see you at the address you already have, which is only a short taxi ride from your hotel."

Mentally cursing, Jingles replied, "Sorry, Petal, but I cannot leave at the moment as I am awaiting an urgent call which is impossible to redirect, so do you mind meeting me here?"

The response was terse and to the point. "So, you are stuck in the Oak Bar, I suppose. I will be there shortly."

Twenty minutes later, Richard was pleasantly offended when an elegantly garbed, handsome female brunette of around thirty years old wended her way to his table and sat down with a pointed lack of any formal greeting. "Well, Jingles, I must say your official photograph certainly flatters you, but goodness me, you do seem to be doing extravagantly well for yourself."

Her victim was far from deflated and roundly responded, "You really look extremely young to hold one rank above me as a major, Petal, and I am staying in the Plaza as a result of my proper job. What's your poison?"

Judging by the lady's decidedly unfriendly manner, the reply was no surprise. "I will have an orange juice and you can cut out the flannel as, from what I have gleaned from your file, you embody everything that I despise in a male. Had you reported to my office, as I should have ordered you to do, you would have discovered that it adjoins my highly fashionable 3rd Avenue dress shop, which happens to be my proper job."

Whilst Petal's provocateur ordered a personal refill, plus her dreary beverage, he mused to himself, *in a minute, I expect she is going to tell me that if I was the last man in the world, she would never marry me. Anyway, in spite of*

THREE

her bolshiness, she really is quite a corker with everything apparently in the right place.

Large hazel eyes then aggressively fixed upon Richard. "You do realise that your crazy vendetta is out of the question, don't you? Your intentions totally cut across my policies so far as Noraid is concerned, where a degree of diplomacy is necessary and has proved to achieve useful results in the past. Whether you approve or not, hordes of your American allies and friends, especially in this city and Boston, are pro-Irish."

Blake's response was passionate as he leaned closer to Petal for emphasis. "Are you trying to tell me that a stinking murdering animal like Liam Riley cannot be culled because of your obsequious diplomacy?"

The response was categorical. "Listen, Captain Blake, I fully realise that this person is a dangerous, vile psychopath. However, I know my home territory and am totally confident that his unwelcome presence will not be tolerated for long by certain operatives with whom I am acquainted within the Noraid hierarchy. So, Captain, as you have already been kind enough to highlight your inferior rank, I forbid you to take any unilateral action concerning Riley's future. If you decide to make yourself useful to our cause without jeopardising your real job and flashy lifestyle, do not hesitate to let me know."

With that, the petulant lady gracefully departed, having barely quaffed her drink, leaving Richard feeling frustrated but also reluctantly impressed and more than a little fascinated!

Then, following his securing some advice from the waiter on the most exciting night spots to visit, a plump, middle-aged, balding fellow in a snug double-breasted blue suit sat down at his table.

Blake had already vaguely noticed this person sitting at the bar and, being aware of the American tendency to be overfamiliar, was only mildly offended by his intrusion.

"Hi, Englishman, let me get you another shot, and forget that waiter's recommendation, as the Studio 54 nightclub is full of schmucks and perverts, plus, on a Friday, you will certainly have to wait in line to get into the joint."

Accepting his offer of another cocktail, Richard enquired of his new drinking partner, "So, how come you are an expert night owl? You look like a family man."

In reply, the intruder slid a NYPD badge across the tabletop, identifying him as Detective Sergeant Buck Kean and intoned, "You really oughta get your pissed-off girlfriend to keep her voice down. I hardly needed my sonic enhancer to follow every word of your highly interesting conversation just now."

With that, as Buck pulled a black plastic spying device out of his pocket, Richard aggressively grunted, "So, what gives then?"

The glib response was, "Dead simple, Mr Jingles, or should I call you the lowly Captain Blake? Unlike your reluctant local allies, I wish to assist you in achieving your totally justified mission."

"So, why in God's name would that be, Sergeant?"

THREE

The policeman's baggy, bloodshot eyes continued to focus intently upon Richard whilst he took a swift swig of his beer.

"Because, although I am of Irish stock, I cannot bear to see the police's 'hands-off' policy with Noraid enabling a punk who is guilty of murder in the UK to freely walk around my city. What you also have to understand is that, unlike your home police force, in this city, at least we endeavour to monitor all our undercover mavericks and that includes the FBI rats."

Although he was unconvinced by the ingenuous simplicity of Kean's justification, Blake pursued the matter further. "So, what assistance do you envisage bringing to my table?"

Scratching his dandruff-peppered balding pate whilst he requested another drink, the police officer went on to qualify his offer.

"The good news is that, like your bitchy girl suggested just now, the Noraid guys are far from enamoured with being stuck with Riley's presence. As such, they won't have him hanging around their main residence by the downtown dock's Pier 57, and my contact tells me that they are moving him to a separate location today, which I will not be aware of until until tomorrow morning. Assuming, via his distinct lack of friends, that he will then be on his own, this presents a perfect opportunity for you to strike.

My precinct station house is bang next to the Rockefeller Centre, just off mid-town Fifth Avenue, where I am willing to discretely meet you tomorrow at 2pm in our small parking lot and fill you in with Riley's new address details. How about that for a supportive gesture?"

On receiving a hesitant affirmative response, the bluff police officer gulped down the rest of his beer, remarking as he stood up to leave, "Must get home to the wife and kids. However, before leaving, I have to say that as you are now serving in a more furtive capacity, you should only wear double-breasted suits as that gun you are toting sticks out like a rapist's dick to anyone who knows the name of the game."

In spite of Jingles finding the departing policeman more than a little repugnant, he had certainly served up an opportunity that was sufficiently tempting to be seriously considered.

Nevertheless, as Richard then grabbed a snack in the hotel's Oyster Bar and opted for an early night, the profound words of Major Lawson, his OC at Officer Cadet school were praying on his mind. "If something appears to be too good to be true, then it probably is, and naive officers inevitably fill many graves!"

The next morning, with time to kill before his police appointment, Jingles decided that, should his strategies turn out to be unviable, he should try to salvage his credibility with Petal, in view of their truly abortive first meeting.

Also, via his basic, lascivious nature, he felt an urge to be in her presence again.

There was no way, however, that he intended to mention his mysterious encounter with the police sergeant after her departure from the Oak Bar the evening before.

THREE

Her address, 620, Third Avenue was indeed bang next door to a clearly stylish and fashionable lady's boutique and, on failing to raise any response by sounding the front doorbell, Blake entered the shop.

"Well, a questionable surprise indeed, Captain, are you here to apologise?" was the elegant major's greeting, to which a suitably obsequious response was fielded.

"Ma'am, I cannot bear our being at loggerheads and am deeply sorry if I was boorish last night. I have never claimed to be a skilful fence mender, but in your case, I shall make a special effort."

Petal then actually smiled, which transformed her finely boned features into glowing perfection.

"Having now had a word with McCarthy concerning our encounter, I believe that might be a superlatively good idea.

Sally, be a darling and bring coffee with all the trimmings to my office for me and Captain Blake, after which, please take care of any customers. We should not be that long."

With that, she ushered her guest into a comfortable small drawing room to the rear of the boutique.

As they settled into comfortable armchairs whilst refreshments were neatly laid out on an adjacent small table, the major opened the conversation in a sympathetic tone.

"I now comprehend the vigour of your vengeful intentions as I understand from Falcon that Riley's murder method was somewhat over the top. I also gather that, in your typical style, you were romantically involved with the victim."

Richard could not avoid filling his saucer with coffee, as he slammed his freshly filled cup down on the table.

"What! 'Somewhat over the top'. Is that how that unfeeling bastard described Riley's unspeakable actions? I will tell you exactly how the sick animal carried out his sadistic crime."

Then, in a passion of bitter remembrance, he described, with no holds barred, the full gory details of the slaying, before adding, as he slumped back in his seat, "And yes, I was extremely fond of the sweet, misguided lady."

In an attempt to defuse the harsh tension of the moment, Petula murmured, "You should not be so hard on our revered Falcon; his Bach is far worse than his Wagner."

As they both burst into semi-hysterical laughter, Richard observed that tears of sympathy were welling up in those beautiful big brown eyes, which meant that his superior officer's perfect body most probably possessed a heart.

Having then lit a cigarette for them both, the lady carried on, "However, I am sorry to say that your 'unfeeling bastard' and I agree that if you are determined to pursue an independent course, we can have nothing to do with it. Nevertheless, if you are prepared to collaborate with me and my agents in developing a subtle plan of action, we will do our utmost to assist you in achieving your objective."

Blake stood up and made to leave. "Thanks a bunch, your vague rhetoric reminds me of my army days."

However, as he moved towards the door, Petula grabbed his arm. "Dick, if you are determined to go it alone, I do now understand why, but for Christ's sake

THREE

be careful. Also, whatever you do, involve no renegade Irish compatriots, of which there is an abundance, to assist you with carrying out your probably underplanned mission. I am now totally conversant with the scene here and, although the Irish are ever charming, generous and amusing, there is a contingent of them who will stop at nothing to defend what they see as their beleaguered patriotism. If someone is perceived as any form of threat to the cause, they are likely to be snuffed out like a candle."

Having delivered her ominous warning, Petula then accepted a peck on her proffered cheek as Richard took his leave but would have been horrified had she been aware of his imminent appointment!

However, following his departure, she did become irritated with herself that, for the second time, the presence of this arrogant man that she hardly knew had triggered an erotic moist sensation in her most intimate bodily region.

FOUR

As Detective Kean huddled in the least exposed zone of his precinct's parking lot, wishing that he had worn an overcoat on such a freakishly chilly autumn day, his mind drifted back to fond and bitter memories of his father. Fond, because he had been a generous, loving parent and bitter because, in 1936 he was cruelly cut down by the UK's 'Belfast Specials'.

However, his morbid reflections were quickly dispelled by the arrival of his stool pigeon. "So, there you are, Captain Jingles. Not only have you jeopardised my career by checking me out over the phone before I got in this morning, but also, you turn up ten minutes late. I am fucking freezing so, as all this is highly confidential, we will sneak off to a quiet little bar that I know."

Richard eagerly agreed and followed the policeman's lumbering form to a decidedly down-market local den where, on arrival, his host purchased a couple of lagers and ushered him to a table in a cramped alcove.

"OK, Chuck, what have you got to tell me?"

FOUR

Assailing the captain with his foul breath in their confined surroundings, the detective then launched into succinct report. "The situation is very straightforward: Riley has effectively been isolated and is now obliged to exist in a run-down apartment which is located in the basement of 60, Pine Street, a major office complex in the city's financial district. As the neighbouring flats are unoccupied, after work hours all sounds of whatever magnitude are unlikely to be heard by anybody, if you know what I mean."

In spite of the spittle which punctuated his dialogue, the policeman's information appeared to be most encouraging.

"Just one other thing, sergeant: as the home is located in an office complex, what about access?"

"Well, sir, the building's main reception area does not go into a restricted mode with guards, etcetera, until nine-thirty in the evening. Before that, although there is usually a token receptionist on duty, anyone can just walk in. So far as the actual apartment is concerned, as it is apparently in such a dilapidated state, I am certain the door will prove to be but a flimsy barrier. You will obviously employ your tried-and-tested military judgement, but I would have thought that around six-thirty tonight might be a good time to strike."

"Great; that could not be clearer and thanks a million. Let me buy you the other half before I have to leave, or would you prefer something a little stronger?"

The reply was somewhat of a relief. "Neither, Captain, I really must get back to the 'cop shop' before I get dropped in the shit."

As Chuck was then ascending the dive's steep steps following his exit, he breathlessly murmured to himself, "One born every minute!"

***

For the first time since his arrival in New York, Liam Riley was beginning to regain his brutal confidence.

Apart from the man presently in his flat, who was equally dangerous, every one of his so-called fellow patriots had treated him like a leper since his arrival in New York, culminating in his being confined to a clapped-out dump of an apartment.

Nevertheless, isolation had suited his obsessive determination to humiliate and destroy the Englishman who epitomised everything he detested and had not only stolen his woman but also had the gall to be intent upon executing him.

He poured his companion another whiskey. "Hey, Pat, are we sure that the iron ring we have rigged in the ceiling will bear human weight? He is quite a big bastard, you know."

"Yeah, of course it's kosher. To you, Liam, everyone is a big bastard," was Mr O'Rafferty's unkind response to his squat compatriot.

"You are a mouthy fucker, Pat, but I will let you off this time as you are about to be of use to me. Anyway, whatever you say, I am not nearly as compact as Captain Blake will be by the time I have finished with him. I hope that you have your baseball bat to hand as Uncle Chuck reckoned he might be getting here at six-thirty or so and that is around now."

***

After Richard had furtively stolen along a musty subterranean corridor with some difficulty, due to his newly purchased heavy boots, his first kick burst the door to apartment U3 wide open. Calamitously, though, on then rushing in – before he could open fire at his quarry who was leering at him from a sofa – his senses were violently extinguished.

On regaining consciousness shortly thereafter, Blake found himself bereft of his clothing and suspended from the ceiling with handcuffs biting into his wrists whilst his bound feet were barely touching the floor.

To exacerbate the horror of the moment, the stunted lout who was obviously Riley was strutting around him with a cigarette dangling from his smirking lips and a maniacal glint in his piercing grey eyes.

"Well, Captain arsehole of the year, I trust you like the pretty bracelets that your new pal, my uncle Chuck, gave me for you to wear. Although you did not perform very well when playing baseball with my mate Pat just now, as you are a thoroughbred English turd, you are probably a keen sportsman. Thus, in the interests of fairness, I have sent Pat home, which means that I do not now have to share the competitive fun that you and I are about to enjoy with anyone else. My speciality is bare-knuckle boxing, so I hope you won't mind if I demonstrate this talent when I have extinguished my cigarette."

Following which, the bully experienced a twinge of irritation when the grinding out of his smouldering butt into his victim's navel produced not so much as a whimper.

This was then followed by a rain of expertly delivered punches to Richard's upper body and face, which produced some involuntary pained grunts as his nose and several ribs were fractured and two teeth were spat from his copiously bleeding mouth.

Then, standing back to nurse his now bruised knuckles, his tormentor muttered, "I believe that the time has now come to forget the Marquis of Queensbury's rules," as he launched into a series of vicious kicks with his hobnailed boots.

These focused upon Blake's knees and groin, who, following some agonised cries, managed to defiantly intone in spite of his mangled mouth, "Is that all that you can manage, you pathetic little coward?"

With that, Riley stepped back and, going to a small nearby table, produced an eight-inch cooking knife from a draw. "Far from it; I have a major treat in store for you before I allow you to smoulder in hell. By the way, this blunt hacker will not be anything like as efficient as your electric carving knife, with which I cut off Rose's tits and fingers before blowing her brains out. I shall now surgically deprive you of the appendages via which, by pouring your vile pus into the stupid bitch, you somehow converted her into becoming a traitor to me and my cause."

There are sometimes periods in one's life when all appears to be completely lost; then, at the last moment, a redeeming miracle occurs. It was now Richard's turn to receive such a blessing.

FOUR

As his assaulter's horrendous intent was about to commence, the flat's already-shattered door crashed open and an armed 'ghost' burst in. "Liam! What the fuck are you up to now? Where is this guy's gun?"

As he was obviously in awe of this unexpected caller, Riley cautiously responded, "Tony, what a pleasant surprise to see you, especially as I am just about to perform an overdue duty. His pistol is over there with his clothing."

Without another word, the intruder crossed the room, grabbed the Beretta and shot the stocky killer between the eyes.

Then, having retrieved the hand cuff keys from the corpse's pocket, he cut down a now barely conscious Jingles, who just managed to croak, "You are supposed to be dead."

"That is a nice way to greet an old mate who has just saved your arse as a long overdue thank you for once saving mine. Congratulations on escaping from my little shit of a Noraid colleague. Your bumping him off will not break too many hearts! Great to see you again after so long, but you must learn to take care of your teeth, and for God's sake get that snout straightened. Now, let's get you to a hospital."

***

Blake's journey was a remote experience, blurred by the agony of his recently inflicted wounds, but he was aware of the fact that at some point his 'ghostly' saviour absconded.

Instant sedation upon his infirmary arrival then mercifully drugged him into a deep sleep until he was awakened the following afternoon by a benevolent middle-aged man in a spotless white coat. "Welcome to the Memorial Stone Kettering Hospital. I am Doctor Richard Sykes and will be responsible for your restorative treatment whilst you are with us. First of all, though, Ms Petula Larkin popped in this morning and gave me this letter on the strict understanding that I ensure you read it before conversing with anyone. As I am an honest man and she was a delightful lady, if you feel up to it, why not do so now?"

On taking the proffered envelope, Blake opened it with some difficulty, due to the state of his wrists, and withdrew a note which simply read:

IDIOT. Walking from the Pierre Hotel to the Plaza across Central Park at 8pm. No wonder you got mugged!

Screwing the slip of paper into a ball, Richard turned to the doctor and articulated with difficulty, "Just a bollocking for getting mugged in Central Park. Women!"

The medic smiled knowingly. "Bloody women, indeed. Can't live with them; can't live without them. Anyway, this one is very keen to see you and, now that someone has booked you into one of our most luxurious private rooms, I am allowing her to call in at eight-thirty tomorrow morning. As you are clearly a gentleman, I would not dream of mentioning your financial status, but a cursory examination whilst you were out for the count suggests that some remedial surgery will be called for. Whilst your nose obviously needs attention and two compound-fractured ribs must be straightened out, I am concerned over the sorry state of your left knee which has severe cartilage laceration. Your deep wrist chafing is a total mystery to me, but my main concern is the extreme pummelling that your testicles have suffered, where I shall not be able to assess the extent of the damage until the bruising subsides. Anyway, the need to replace two of your teeth is a relatively simple matter, which can be taken care of by an orthodontist friend of mine whilst you are recuperating here."

The patient attempted some humour with difficulty. "Apart from all that, I am in good shape, then?"

The consultant smiled humourlessly. "Please try not to speak with your mouth in that state. I find that the most extraordinary aspect of your extreme misfortune is that, whilst you have been the victim of one of the most savage muggings in which I have ever been involved, your watch, signet ring and gold cuff links, plus the contents of your wallet, remained intact. This, of course, means that the motive for your attack is far from clear, unless one assumes that your assailants were in some way interrupted.

Anyway, I will leave now, but I almost forgot to tell you about a call my PA received from Ms Larkin an hour ago. Apparently, she contacted your London boss, one Mr Wellington-Green, and it would appear that he is already on his way over here to see you. If that's OK, just nod your head."

Blake nodded his head with some difficulty, as he was endeavouring to consume, via a tube, some liquid nourishment which was being proffered by a perky young blonde nurse.

When agent Petal entered the hospital room the following morning, she was unable to mask her expression of shocked horror on viewing Richard's battered, bandaged and strapped-up condition.

Nonetheless, although those gorgeous eyes were brimming once again, she was determined to maintain her contempt for what she correctly considered to be his crass irresponsibility.

"In view of the fact that Doctor Sykes has told me that you should not be using what appears left of your mouth, which at least obviates the probability of my being harangued by your bullshit, I shall speak my mind, just once. As you are infamous for your persistent military indiscipline, maybe you have now learnt your lesson at last for deliberately disobeying the orders of a superior officer, which on this occasion happened to be me! Having now got the full story from your saviour, it should have been obvious to anyone but a brainless moron that the cop was setting you up. Had it not occurred to you that he was one of those blindly loyal Irish patriots that I specifically warned you to avoid?

Apart from that, an elementary check on the sergeant's family background would have revealed the fact that his father was killed by the Brits and that the vile sadist you were pinpointing was his nephew."

Following this passionate diatribe, the lady collapsed on the ample bed in floods of tears.

The accused then just managed a lisping response. "You are dead right, and I am most contrite, but where the hell did Tony Price come from?"

FOUR

Having then swiftly recovered her composure as she dabbed her eyes with a silk hanky, Petula seated herself on a bedside chair and solemnly responded, "Well, that is where your devil's luck saved you. Mr Price was… and I repeat *was*… our top Noraid agent. However, thanks to your predicament causing him to disobey orders, his continuance in this role has now become inviable. His specific instructions from me had been that if you made any unauthorised moves which put you in jeopardy, matters must be allowed to run their course in order to preserve his Noraid credibility. However, notwithstanding this, because during your colonial service in Africa, you courageously averted his death, he felt obliged to rescue you, regardless.

Although we are still fairly certain that Noraid believe that it was you who shot Riley, Tony – code name 'Plotter' – is now in semi-cold storage, and I certainly will not allow him to visit you here. To regain some shred of operational credibility with me when you can speak properly again, I would appreciate your recounting the details of how you boldly saved his neck in Africa all those years ago."

At this point, the door to the room was flung open to reveal the immaculate form of Toby Wellington-Green, complete with red carnation, who instantly boomed, "I can hardly believe it, Dick, you get horribly duffed up by a bunch of louts in the park, probably for some form of romantic indiscretion, then here you are a day and a half later with a strikingly beautiful lady sitting by your bed!"

Ms Larkin was in no mood for 'laddish' comments of this nature, so with a terse, "Don't speak, Richard; I will be in touch later," she squeezed past the ebullient new visitor and departed without attempting to introduce herself.

Having remarked, "Well, I got that right!" the flamboyant executive set down one of those bottles of a vintage malt whiskey that are so rare no one has ever heard of them, before taking a closer look at his battered friend. "God, but you look bloody dreadful, and I apologise for my frivolous comments just now as you are probably extremely lucky to still be alive. As I plan to be around for a while to cheer you up and monitor your progress, I have taken over your Plaza junior suite. Right now, though, as the doc has limited my visit to ten minutes, I must cover some important points with you immediately.

First of all, as mentioned during our last meeting in my office, I did not believe that you had been fully freed from military duties when you came to work for me. Don't forget that I am a long-term friend of your last CO Bill Barnham who, in spite of being ever critical of your lack of personal discipline, very much admired your outstanding basic soldierly abilities. His praises also included your exceptional instinctive skills during covert missions, where I understand that you made quite a name for yourself in East Germany and Hong Kong. As a result of Bill's plaudits, and because I am a nosey bugger, I decided to carry out some checking via my political connections.

I know that you were as over the moon as I was when the pipe-faced taxation maniac Wilson was booted out in June and our lot got back in, even if it was sadly under the deadly dull Ted Heath. I am sure that you are also well aware that Roger Muswell has taken over as

FOUR

Home Secretary, which now makes him responsible for monitoring and controlling the secret service brigade, of which you now appear to be part.

What you probably don't know is that, in addition to being on my holding company board, Roger also happens to have a country home next door to my Redstone Manor House in Surrey. As such, he has become a close acquaintance of mine and recently came to supper, when I encouraged him to be a tad indiscrete over the brandies. I am therefore fully aware of your links with MI6 and in no doubt whatsoever that your recent misadventure relates in some way to this involvement.

Notwithstanding that, as I have limited time and you can obviously only converse with difficulty, let me have a note when I pop in tomorrow re your progress, if any, on the Gilles Barton front. Securing the Mark Lines fleet would provide a somewhat needed boost to your commercial credibility with certain board members and, if you hook the fish, I am happy to help you land it, particularly if it necessitates a trip to New Orleans."

***

The following three weeks turned out to be a pleasant, much-needed upswing in the fortunes of Captain Jingles.

Doctor Sykes appeared to be fully satisfied with the results of his treatment, and even though his opinion upon the extent of Richard's groin damage remained non-committal, he was at least verging upon being optimistic.

Meanwhile, Gilles, as a typical politician, had adopted a position of national guilt over the fact that an esteemed English friend and visitor to the USA had been savagely abused by American hooligans in a municipal park.

He was also totally smitten by the aristocratic Toby and the two of them were imminently scheduled to visit Mark Lines in New Orleans with a view to securing the impending renewal placement of their fleet's full insurance programme.

However, it was an offer from Petula, during the most recent of her rather rare visits, which ultimately put the cherry onto Blake's cake.

"Well, Dick, as I understand that you have to be available for out-patient treatment following your forthcoming discharge, rather than languishing in a stuffy hotel, why not come to stay at my place until you have fully recovered?"

As this just had to be what is now commonly known as a 'no-brainer', the eager invitee's response was, "Petula, I consider that to be a brilliant idea and am overjoyed to accept your generous offer."

FIVE

On responding to the bell, Ms Larkin was pleasantly surprised to find Tony Price standing at her doorway one Sunday morning. "Plotter! Wonderful to see you. As it appears to be after twelve, do come in and have a drink."

Having settled him down in her drawing room with a tankard of ale, she questioned her unexpected guest. "Well, how are things in the Noraid zoo? We have been worried about you."

After taking a swig of his beer, Price responded, "For a start, I am here to tell you that I have been suddenly recalled to London by old McCarthy to perform an apparently urgent mission and am due to be on my way tomorrow afternoon. This is somewhat of a relief so far as my position at Noraid is concerned because their suspicion of my involvement with the Riley slaying is becoming rifer by the day, mainly as a result of too many police noses in the pot. Uncle Chuck appears to be determined to root out the specific person who topped his charming nephew. By the way, how is Blake doing?"

With a wee tingle in her tummy, Petula volunteered, "Amazingly well in the circumstances, in fact, he is coming to stay here during his provisional discharge on Tuesday."

Much to the lady's annoyance, a sarcastic, "Oh yeah," was the response.

"Oh yeah, nothing, Plotter. Apart from the fact that he is definitely not my type at all, I find your long-term companion to be far too full of himself. You are bad enough, but as I keep forgetting to ask him, how exactly did Dick manage to save your life?"

Price chuckled. "Ah, so it's 'Dick' now, is it? Give me another beer and I will tell you."

With a swiftly refilled pewter receptacle in his hand, he continued, "Dick and I first met in 1959 on a plane from London to Kano in Nigeria. We were both youthful, fairly recently commissioned colonial secondments and, as prop planes take forever, we got so shit-faced during a Benghazi stop-over that we had to be removed from the wrong plane on re-embarking."

This snippet failed to generate any feminine mirth.

"Anyway, by far the most important VI P in Northern Nigeria was the Sardauna of Sokoto, Sir Ahmadu Bello, who was based in Kaduna and considered to be the country's top Muslim. Not only was he very pro UK and therefore a stabilising influence in the build-up to Nigerian Independence in 1960, but also, he later became the country's Northern President. The fly in the ointment was that, like most Hausas, he hated the mainly Christian and more Westernised Igbo tribe, who would eventually murder him during their early Biafran coup attempt in 1966.

"However, Dick and I were put in charge of a squad whose mission it was to covertly thwart the first Igbo assassination attempt in December '59. The vital need for total secrecy was to obviate the Sardauna employing dramatic public retaliatory action, whilst also avoiding disruption to Britain's necessary close relationship with the Igbos, who held many native government positions. Failure of the operation was not an option, and we were on our own if anything went wrong. Fortunately, as it turned out, we split our squad in two and I went in to dispense with the hitmen whilst the Blake team contained their reserves.

"However, I had been betrayed by one of my Yoruba tribe corporals and, during a violent hand-to-hand scuffle, my loyal half-dozen men were cut to pieces with machetes whilst I was strung up to be hanged from a tree. Blake then arrived on the scene just in time and, as he was heavily outnumbered, ignored our instructions to be discrete by ordering his men to immediately open up with their Sten guns. In spite of his taking a bullet in his right arm and three of his men being shot dead, Richard managed to induce a cowardly surrender from the Igbo squad. The result was that my head maintained its normal distance from my shoulders after all. So, Petal, now do you blame me for rescuing him from that creature's tender mercies?"

"Well, it appears to be a typical quid pro quo. He disobeyed orders to rescue you and you repaid him in kind!"

***

Petula's anticipated next visitor arrived in a yellow cab from the hospital at 12.30pm the following Tuesday, complete with a bulging suitcase.

"Dick, you are looking much better and far neater in smart casual attire; crumpled pyjamas really do very little for one's image. Leave your case in the hall and come on through so that we can have a chat over a spot of lunch."

With an enthusiastic, "Hi, Petal. Absolutely wonderful to see you," her guest did as he was told and followed her into a large, luxurious kitchen/diner where a small table was laid for two with an ice bucket on hand which contained a bottle of Italian Peria del Mar.

After they were both seated, the hostess apologetically volunteered, "Because of the state of your mouth, I am serving you some boring old chicken soup, followed by a cheese and tomato omelette. I am delighted to see that your missing teeth have been immaculately replaced. Also, your reconstructed nose looks great now that the swelling following the operation has at last subsided. How are your other bits?"

As he proceeded to open the wine, Blake responded nonchalantly, "Well, ribs are ribs and take their time in mending, as I have discovered through breaking so many via my sporting activities. Unfortunately, though, my right knee is still pretty stiff…"

Petula cut in, "Don't worry about having to use stairs whilst you are staying here; I have an elevator that can waft you up to your bedroom floor."

FIVE

The reply to this was somewhat of a humorous gamble. "Actually, I need elevating in another battered and far more important part of my body where stiffness appears to have infuriatingly, but hopefully only temporarily, deteriorated!"

Snatching up her now filled glass with a wry grin on her face, the target of this over-mischievous observation roundly responded, "Captain Jingles, you are, as ever, incorrigible. Nevertheless, when Tony Price dropped in en route to London last Sunday, he recounted the details of how you heroically saved his life, which I did find impressive. So much so that I am now prepared to treat you with a modicum of respectful tolerance in the future."

Maintaining the more relaxed mood of the conversation, as the soup was being prepared, Dick ventured into story time.

"That was all about stopping the Igbo dissidents knocking off poor old Sokoto, who they eventually managed to brutally knobble seven years later, anyway. I knew the patriarchal paragon of eccentricity personally as he was totally obsessed with watching rugby. When there was a match in Kaduna, he would turn up in either a Rolls or a Cadillac – courtesy of the UK taxpayer – and jump up and down screaming like a schoolboy on the touchline throughout the game. Then, on one occasion, when he had been particularly impressed by a 'seven-a-side' tournament, he invited all the players back to his vast palatial home – also courtesy of the UK taxpayer – and served us half pint tumblers of neat scotch, which were presented on silver trays by a host of cutlass-bearing, pantalooned and turbaned flunkies. Needless to say, with all that booze flowing, things soon got distinctly out of hand so, when we tried to storm what we believed was the harem zone, salvers were abandoned whilst swords were drawn, and we were unceremoniously prodded and chased back to our cars by the erstwhile whiskey waiters!"

When the two of them had finished laughing and were getting stuck into their meal, Richard rounded off by querying, "So what is the score with Tony? I have seen nothing of him since the fateful night, but, as you have already told me, his role in Noraid has become decidedly less tenable?"

"Indeed, you are dead right there, Dick, but all I know is that he was flying over to London for a meeting with Falcon, who apparently has a new project for him to get to grips with. Incidentally, why were you so firmly under the impression that he was already dead?"

Richard adopted a perplexed expression. "His gruesome demise has been an army presumption for years as a lesson to all for what can happen if you desert your post. As he originally only held a three-year Short Service Commission, on falling in love with the dashing, rugged qualities of soldiering in Africa, he returned to England for training to qualify him for being a full-term Regular Officer. Having done so, the powers that be then totally ignored his request for African service and posted him to Frankfurt, which was infamous for tedious garrison duties. As a result of this, and in a presumed fit of pique, he then astounded everyone by deserting in Paris, having signed up as a mercenary to support the Congo Republic's

FIVE

Katanga rebels. On then being taken prisoner by the Congolese, following an aborted ambush, it was alleged on reliable authority that his captors arbitrarily spit roasted him to death for a laugh. As an old friend of his, I am obviously delighted to learn that this did not occur, but what do his records say and how the hell did he get into our game?"

Petal perked up with alacrity. "Well, it so happens that I have just completed rereading our file on him which mentions that he was, indeed, based in the Congo up until '62. However, this was as an MI6 agent, where his duty was to report upon the actions of Rene Faulques, a French subversive schemer who was assisting Belgian Fascists to disrupt the ex-colony in order to reoccupy its rich copper and cobalt-bearing zones. In order to justify the myth that Tony was a Katanga supporter, the 'barbequed mercenary' story was obviously fabricated as a cover-up when he was withdrawn after completing his Faulques mission. He has only been over here for just over a year."

Richard burst into laughter. "So, the crafty bastard must have been secretly recruited into MI6 on receiving his regular commission. I have never really trusted people with red hair, particularly if they are taller than me!"

"Never mind, now that you have been resculpted, you are better looking than he is again," was his hostess's benign response.

Following this encouraging observance, the repast was concluded with fruit and cheese, after which, whilst Richard was testing his new gnashers by consuming an apple, Petula suddenly looked at her watch.

"Christ, Dick, whilst sitting here relaxing with you, I totally forgot that I have given my assistant, Sally, the afternoon off, so I must leave and take care of the shop immediately. So sorry to rush off like this and I am afraid that Tuesday is a late seven-thirty closing day."

As she hurriedly departed, her new guest called after her, "Proper jobs must always come first, Major. I will get the catering company that has recently been subsidising my hospital diet to spoil us with a snack at around eight-fifteen."

Blake then spent a mundane afternoon, occasionally reading and half-watching television, whilst his hostess vigorously vended her boutique's overpriced wares next door. Therefore, the sumptuous feast that was wheeled in by two liveried employees of 'Ever Succulent' just after 8pm could not have been a more welcome surprise for Petula.

Nonetheless, as the two of them relaxed, enjoying their liqueurs on a sofa following caviar, steak au poivre and crepe suzettes, embraced by Pouilly Fuisse and Chateau Margaux, Richard was finding it difficult to savour the moment.

He reluctantly realised that this sense of unease was caused by anxiety over his ability to perform during what would normally have been the romantic phase of the evening.

"Dick, this is delicious, but it is the weirdest brandy that I have ever tasted."

As he could now sense the warmth of the lady's thigh pressing against his, this unsophisticated query was bizarrely welcome.

FIVE

"That, my dear Petula, is because you are quaffing a fabulous Bayeux creation: Calvados, which has bestowed far more enjoyment upon civilised humanity than the tapestries ever did. Unlike cognac, it has nothing to do with grapes and is a blessing for which we have to thank the common apple. I thought it might make a pleasant change, but it seems to be having a strange effect upon the shadow of my former self."

Swiftly switching her growing feeling of frustration to one of sympathy, Petula grabbed Dick's hand.

"Oh, you poor fellow, here I am wallowing in your Calvados, having relished the scrumptious supper that you so cleverly organised, whilst selfishly overlooking the fact that you have only just got out of hospital. I shall take you up and put you to bed immediately."

Most unexpectedly, this was not to be. "No, Petal, you have already told me where my bedroom is, and I unpacked and sorted out my stuff this afternoon."

With that, having pecked his unsatisfied hostess on the nose and wished her goodnight, with guilty regret, he ascended to his room in the elevator.

Of the two of them, Petula was by far the most exasperated and, during a sleepless, increasingly frantic night of tossing and turning in her bed, she frequently intimately caressed her body and eventually made a vow of intent for the following morning. Via any depraved and uninhibited means that may be necessary, she was determined to ensure that her house guest fully satiated her body's erotic cravings.

As Richard gradually awoke, he became aware of a fine aroma of exotic scent, which was heavily tinged with the deliciously spicy animalistic tang of female arousal.

On opening his eyes, he was overwhelmed by the close proximity to his face of a lightly furred pink nether vista of moist femininity, which was then suddenly replaced by a brown-eyed, pink-lipped panting vision that hungrily tongued deeply into his already-gasping mouth.

With all concerns of his injuries dispelled by throbbing, rigid desire, he mounted and locked into Petula's pulsating needs for the first of numerous varied orgasmic bondings.

It was not until around midday that his now abundantly satisfied new lover cheekily remarked, "Well, I suppose all that crème de la crème perfection is worth my being court-martialled for seducing a subordinate officer!"

***

Whilst his old friend was recovering from his injuries via intimate recuperative therapy, Price had frustratingly become stranded in a Waldorf Hotel single room, awaiting a summons from Colonel McCarthy.

Eventually, on the morning of the third day after his supposedly urgent arrival in London, he was ordered over the telephone to attend the main MI6 bureau for a 9am meeting with the great man himself.

As he had only been invited to this hallowed location once before, he correctly assumed that the intended subject for discussion must be one of top priority.

On his arrival at Falcon's office, he was peremptorily ordered to be seated in an adjacent virtual classroom by

FIVE

the colonel, who he was surprised to observe was clad in full dress uniform, complete with an impressive row of medals.

"No 'mufti' today, Plotter. Got to see the amateurs this afternoon. Now, sit down at the desk with a notepad on it and pay full attention to my briefing. I may ask you some questions, but you are not allowed to ask me any until I have finished."

Price was then made to feel rather like Richard Burton in a war film as McCarthy uncovered a large wall map of the world and picked up a wooden pointer with which he then proceeded to slap and prod the zones to which he was referring.

"Your mission's big picture is all about the deteriorating stability and reliability of the areas of the world via which oil and its by-products are sourced today. Whilst the USA utilises the majority of its supply for home consumption, Mexican, North Sea and oriental production is still in its infancy and the Iron Curtain resources are obviously politically vulnerable. Meanwhile, apart from their tendency to apply commercial blackmail, the copious Middle Eastern outlets are continually exposed to revolutionary, political and military upheavals, where the current closure of Suez is a prime example. This means that the development of Nigeria's apparently copiously well-stocked oilfields is now becoming significantly more important."

With that, the tip of the pointer moved to the Congo area. "Now, to be more specific, you cannot see it from there, but I am identifying the newest and, even including the Gambia, by far the smallest country in Africa, Berundi, of which I am certain you have never heard. What?"

On receiving a shake of the head from his pupil, the headmaster continued, "The mini state is probably smaller than Sussex and has only been in existence for a year or so. Mobuto, the Congo's dictator who is about as honest and benevolent as your old Katanga pals, allowed Berundi to be carved out of his country's north-west corner, in exchange for a generous Genevan gift. We strongly suspect the Chinese are heavily involved with this venture but are certain that the driving force behind the territorial creation is a militant Nigerian group of erstwhile Biafrans. Their ultimate aim is to retake and expand General Ojukwu's recently dissolved Biafran State, where, of course, a majority of the Nigerian oilfields are located.

On the face of things, it is hard to envisage that the existence of this minute and somewhat remote mini-nation could pose a threat to Nigerian stability. However, from our sources, we know that a vigorous military recruitment and training programme is currently being pursued at Berundi's large, newly constructed army base and that there is and has been a considerable influx of modern weaponry taking place.

"From information we have gleaned, it would appear that the project's grand design is to create a sophisticated infantry force of up to three thousand men which will eventually be aerially transported to a location along the southern Nigerian/Cameroon border. This substantial echelon will then link up with a similar-sized outfit, which will have been detached from the Nigerian Army

FIVE

by a cross section of traitorous officers who are prepared to support this new Biafran revolution. The next phase of their overall strategy will obviously be to take over, by force of arms if necessary, the oil-rich south-eastern quarter of the nation. Frustratingly, the long-standing Nigerian premier, General Gowan, having finally managed to stabilise his country's upheavals in this area last January, has so far refused to take our warnings of an imminent rebellious resurgence seriously. Part of the reason for his smug confidence is the fact that there is no evidence at all that the now banished but spied upon Ojukwu is involved in any way with subversive activities.

"Nevertheless, I am in constant touch with certain politicians, both in Lagos and the London Nigerian Legation, whom I am vigorously urging to heed our warnings and am glad to say that some of them are beginning to listen. I should mention in passing, a bizarre facet of the new Berundi base is that, presumably as some form of cover-up, a large encampment for the training of specialised male and female slaves is being developed in close proximity to the military area…"

At this point, Price cut in, "No surprise; whatever the progressive modern thinkers choose to believe, the slave trade between Africa and mainly the Middle East is ever present in one form or another. Damn it, when Blake and I were serving in the Frontier Force only ten years ago, it was one of our duties to prevent the practice in—"

"Silence, Plotter. How dare you interrupt when I have told you no questions until I have finished. I was about to add that the Congolese, probably in league with the People's

Republic of China, are believed to be supplying the means for troop and equipment air transportation in exchange for lucrative oil-related deals, but we have no proof of this so far. Unfortunately, our air reconnaissance efforts have now been curtailed via bloody Mobuto reporting us to the UN and stating his right to shoot down all further intruders. Nevertheless, as a destructive upheaval of Nigeria's potentially thriving oil facilities would be a disaster for UK interests, this intended insurrection simply cannot be permitted to occur. What we now urgently need is more precise intelligence concerning the current situation in Berundi, particularly the stage that their development of a trained fighting force has now reached.

In addition to this, we must endeavour to discover the roll and identity of Biafran allies in the Congo, and possibly Cameroon, where so far the latter country has behaved in a typically French fashion by refusing to comment. Also, the extent of Chinese involvement must obviously be fully assessed and quantified.

In view of the fact that your Noraid status is no longer viable, and you are already familiar with this geographical theatre of operation, I am putting you in sole charge of investigating the looming disaster. The primary task of your mission will be to fully evaluate all the aspects of the situation that I have just outlined and seek out any 'Achilles heels' in the rebel's plans for what must be a precariously ambitious venture. Your cover story will be that you are representing Birkbeck Energy – a genuine oil company, based in Guernsey – as you are eager to consummate a deal, which has been already proposed to the would-be controllers of Nigeria's oilfields. The motive for so doing is that your company has so far been arbitrarily excluded from participating in the current oil bonanza by the current Nigerian authorities. Thus, by providing the revolutionaries with financial support, Birkbeck will be generously rewarded when the take-over shortly occurs.

"To proceed, you will contact and work with my agent in Port Harcourt, Brigadier Hassan Fort Lamy. He belongs to the sector of Nigeria's army which is primarily responsible for administration and dispatch, similar to our Royal Army Service Corps, and on your arrival, he will supply you with his latest 'sitrep'. As we cannot entirely trust the Nigerian Military at present, due to the possibility of 'moles', you will base yourself at the partly manned Birkbeck local office. This will allow you to make phone calls, plus code and decode message exchanges in privacy. There has already been some telexed and telephonic communication between our bogus Birkbeck representative in Guernsey, one Robert Steinbeck and the so-called Berundi President, Alfred Unegby. As a result of this, he is now expecting some form of investigatory visit so that terms for the oil company's proposed investment can be finalised. Do not raise any queries with me over this as you will be supplied with a partly mocked-up file which contains all relevant commercial details about which you will need to know. Any questions?"

Clearing his throat in a moderately shocked mode, Plotter succinctly responded. "First of all, sir, what do the Yanks make of all this?"

"Fair point. Typically, they have adopted a hypocritical, pragmatic stance. In spite of the fact that they claim to disapprove of colonialism, they have now taken a view that independent African countries are unstable and untrustworthy. Thus, when dealing with them, they tend to play a waiting game before embracing whoever, by fair means of foul, ends up controlling a zone of available profitability. Obviously, in view of our Commonwealth commitments, to take a similar amoral position is not an option for the UK."

"Fascinating, Colonel. Second point. Apart from the brigadier and his cronies, what personal back-up can I expect to receive on the ground?"

Falcon offered an unfamiliar benign smile. "As you both worked together in this location before and have just had a brief, if distinctly undisciplined, encounter in Manhattan, I consider that Jingles will fit the bill. However, you must keep him away from women, as they seem to addle his judgement, and to assist you in controlling the lascivious devil, I am promoting you to Major. Jingles will follow you out when he is fully fit for duty, which hopefully will be soon, as he is already sufficiently robust to be busy corrupting my senior female officer in New York. Anything else?"

"I shall very much enjoy working with Jingles again, but yes Falcon, I do wish to raise one more point. What's with the Chinese involvement?"

"Well, Major Plotter, as I would have expected you to have already observed, they have been sniffing around in Africa for some years and have maintained a significant presence in Madagascar since 1960. However, in line with Russia's efforts with Kwame Nkrumah's Ghana, their attempts to dominate former colonies have tended to be brushed aside by new independent leaders. Nevertheless, if they could manage to get in on Nigeria's potentially copious energy supplies, this would rank as a national bonanza. Therefore, if as I believe, they have generously invested in Berundi, I am certain that they will also be heavily involved in its weaponry supplies. Having said this, we now come to my main reason for mentioning the slave training complex earlier. Whilst I am pretty certain that Mao Zedong would easily ride out reports of China's combative support for any situation, he would certainly not be comfortable if it became internationally known that the world's ultimate paragon of equality and freedom is in any way involved in the African slave trade. Taiwan's Chiang Kai-shek would have a field day! This could be a key card to play in the future, but as my suppositions are purely based upon conjecture and likelihood, you must urgently establish more tangible data concerning this aspect as a key priority as well.

"For communication via telex with me, you will adopt the same coding structure that was utilised in New York. As Jingles has not yet been made aware of this format, you will familiarise him with it as an urgent priority immediately after he arrives. If that is all, your flight leaves from Heathrow at 0800 hours tomorrow, so pick up your tickets and some money from my ADC, who will also give you a detailed Birkbeck file and keys to their Port Harcourt office."

SIX

Five days later, Richard Blake landed in Port Harcourt's international airport at 3pm, courtesy of American Airlines. In spite of the uncomfortable timing of his JFK flight, he had made the most of his first-class booking since awakening two hours earlier by drowning the recollection of his lover's tearful farewells with a bottle of Krug.

Having then negotiated some rickety steps from the plane and made his way through the distinctly primitive arrivals and baggage claim areas, on his emergence from customs, he was delighted on being greeted by his old friend.

Following warm salutations, Tony then guided him through a chaotic, odorous throng to his five-litre Mercedes SEL which was parked just outside. Richard was relieved to observe that the vehicle was fully air-conditioned as the rank humidity of the atmosphere was already getting to him.

Having stowed his bags in the boot and settled in the front passenger seat, the 'new boy on the block' then asked

SIX

the least urgent of his numerous questions. "Why were you swatting all those blokes in weird uniforms with your ID card as we passed through arrivals just now?"

Tony laughed. "Just sorting out a new antisocial Nigerian tradition. Those bastards masquerade as officials and endeavour to levy bogus 'landing taxes' on naive, well-dressed white guys, with custodial threats if they are refused. The very sight of my diplomatic pass frightens the shit out of them, but I like to give them a clout for their bloody cheek in trying it on. I suppose one could excuse the practice as one of the many unfortunate by-products of independence, but what the hell! I let my chauffeur have a half day off so that I could bring you up to speed as we struggle through the stinking traffic, en route to see Brigadier Hassan Fort Lamy. I am sure you have never heard of him, but he happens to be Falcon's main 'linkman'. Anyhow, as I know you have been told precisely fuck all so far, I will do my best to fill you in, and as the guy we love might say, no questions until I have finished."

Half an hour later, as Richard was endeavouring to fully absorb his convoluted briefing, there was one immediate point that he just had to raise. "Hassan Fort Lamy: I have indeed not heard of him as a brigadier, but I believe that I may have encountered the man as an NCO during my earlier service with you out here. I am sure that you won't remember this, but in the run-up to Independence, I got posted for a short time to run a training company in Zaria. This became necessary because the officer commanding got clobbered with gall stones and the only available replacement was a thick-as-shit Lieutenant, Ernest

Yabuba. One of the platoon sergeants I then inherited was a Hassan Fort Lamy, who, apart from being a sadistic bully, was a total crook. In fact, had it not been for political considerations at the time, I would have had him reduced to the ranks for endeavouring to filch his recruits' savings. I shall be amazed if Falcon has appointed that little shit as our main local contact, so hopefully your one-star general is just another soldier born in Chad with the same name. Nevertheless, as I understand that accelerated promotions to senior rank have not been uncommon in this country since Independence, this may well be the man that I am not eager to meet again, particularly as a superior officer."

At this point, they arrived in Port Harcourt's ramshackle urban precincts where Tony pulled into a squalid car parking area beneath a peeling concrete office block. Then, following a pregnant protracted pause in their conversation as Tony parked up, Richard received a response to his contentious remark.

"Sod it, you have now ruined my day. I have been instinctively uneasy over Fort Lamy's credibility since I arrived out here but just kept telling myself that he must be OK because our clinical governor said so. If our brigadier turns out to be the chap that you have just described, we should now proceed with far greater caution and confine imparting details of our proposed strategies and their implementation to a bare minimum. Nevertheless, as we are about to see Fort Lamy, for Christ's sake do not take the mickey, as he is the only local agent we have to work with for the time being and he tends to be insecure and extremely touchy. The good news is that his boss Major

SIX

General Sammy Okafor is a most charming chap, with a good brain and very much on the ball, in spite of his tendency to be more than a little crafty from time to time."

"Great, Tony, let's roll the ball, and have no fear – I will behave myself."

On arriving at a surprisingly stylish top-floor reception area via a creaky old cage-fronted lift, Richard was pleasantly surprised when they were both warmly greeted by a strikingly attractive young lady, clad in a close-fitting warrant officer's uniform.

Her dark aquiline features burst into a flashing smile as she unwound her shapely long legs, arose from her chair and glided towards them.

"So, Mr Price, this must be your colleague from New York. I trust that your long flight was not too arduous, Mr Blake. I am Company Sergeant Major Cynthia Izanagi and will show both of you into the brigadier right away, as he has another meeting in half an hour."

As they were then being conducted through a heavily panelled door, Richard was struck by the fact that, maybe for security reasons, their military titles were not being used.

Nevertheless, as they entered a spacious office, status considerations did not prevent Blake's former sergeant from blurting out as he manoeuvred his ample frame around his writing table, "I just knew that it had to be Blake the bastard, and I bet that you are probably even more arrogant now than you used to be. Did you know, Mr Price, that your associate gave me a really tough time in Zaria some years ago and even threatened to demote me?"

Richard just had to say something, but then wished that he had not. "Well, Brigadier Fort Lamy, it was probably partly the discipline imposed by me that made you worthy of all your extraordinary promotions ever since!"

The response was maddening. "Not so! Once you Brits had given us our country back, real cream just had to rise to the top."

This remark set the tone of what turned out to be a totally negative meeting where the sneering upstart's scepticism over MI6's assessment of the Berundi situation was the overriding theme, and his early departure was a distinct relief.

Before doing so, however, he did manage to stick an oar into Tony and Richard's plans.

"I am not happy with this private plane ride that has been organised so that both of you can visit the suspects to pursue some obscure ploy of your own. Because you are hardly here in great strength, as your superior officer I am only permitting one of you to make the trip, where I am nominating the most junior and dispensable of the two of you, which happens to be you, Mr Blake."

Further comment was obviated by the entry of Major General Okafor, to whom Fort Lamy hurriedly introduced both of them before rushing off; after which the general immediately ushered them into his vastly superior nearby suite.

As predicted, Sammy Okafor turned out to be a far more charming and civilised officer than his number two and also showed infinitely greater interest in what Price and Blake were endeavouring to achieve.

SIX

Somewhat strangely, though, it soon became apparent that he had managed to eavesdrop their earlier unfriendly encounter with Fort Lamy.

"I am not pressing you to divulge your motives, Richard, but that is an arduously long journey that you are embarking upon tomorrow, which I understand will be in a bit of a toy aeroplane. Incidentally, I believe that it is the remoteness of Berundi's location which is making Brigadier Fort Lamy dubious over the MI6 hierarchy's conclusions. Nevertheless, as he is their nominated agent and your former sergeant, I am certain that his cooperation will continue to be diligent."

This last remark was uttered with a conspiratorial grin before he added, "But, good luck, anyway. If these people's intentions really are what you presume them to be, then they must be thwarted at all costs."

On departing later, following a round of gin and tonics, Richard turned on Tony as they descended in the 'deathtrap' lift. "So, what is all this 'most junior' bollocks, then?"

His friend gave him a deliberately patronising smile. "Oh, didn't I tell you? Falcon upped me to major." Then, as they entered the car park, "And my first order to you in this capacity is that you are not allowed to shag that!"

He was referring to the delectable CSM Cynthia who, on emerging from her dusty red Volkswagen Beetle, immediately hailed them both. "Hey, boys, if you have finished chatting up the scrambled egg brigade, how about taking me for a drink?"

"Why not?" shouted Tony, before murmuring to Jingles, "Please do not get yourself court-martialled!"

Cocktails eventually rolled into a not-too-delicious but extremely entertaining supper in one of the local cafés.

It transpired during their repast that their young companion's exotic appearance emanated from a blend of fine Fulani bone structure and graceful Hausa stature.

However, it was the source of her excellent English that was more fascinating.

Apparently, she and her Nigerian fiancé had gone to live in London a few years earlier, as he had earned a place at Imperial College.

When her young man then dumped her for an ex-Roedean girl, Cynthia was utterly undaunted and with her strikingly beautiful looks and a melodious voice, easily secured a job as a cabaret singer in the Soho Murray's Club.

The substantial money she made paid for a classical crash course at the exclusive Collingham College in Kensington, which sufficiently qualified her for securing a warrant officer status in the Nigerian Army when she returned home.

As the lady concluded the synopsis covering her recent adventures, Richard was bursting to make a comment. "If you were working in Murrays, you may have met my pal Toby, who I know often spends his spare evenings there, especially when his wife is away. In fact, I have accompanied him on his visits to the venue on a couple of occasions myself."

Cynthia responded with nostalgic enthusiasm, "My God, you must be referring to Toby Wellington-Green, who I often sat with and got to know very well. Although a bit old for me, he was still an attractive, highly charming chap who, I believe, ran a Lloyd's insurance outfit of some sort. I am sure that I still have his card somewhere."

Richard was obviously highly tickled by the coincidence. "Well, hang onto it in case you are ever in London again. The man is a fascinating bloke and a close friend of mine with whom I have frequently shared some great times."

Cynthia certainly was quite a girl and wonderful company, but unfortunately their raucous revelry was cut short at 10pm as she had promised to stay over with her mother, who was suffering from a bout of influenza.

Nonetheless, although Dick failed to get an opportunity for earning a court martial, he did establish some vague promises of better things to come!

The unusually early evening actually turned out to be a blessing in disguise as, whilst Richard was checking into the nearby Hilton Hotel, Tony tipsily exclaimed, "Christ Almighty, Dick, I knew there was something I had forgotten. I haven't schooled you in our telex coding system, which Falcon instructed me to urgently do on pain of death, so in spite of your eight-thirty flight tomorrow morning, I am afraid that this must be done straight away. Stick your case in your room and then come to mine, number 362, where I am sure we can fit in a nightcap or two whilst we work. Also, thanks to the Farting Llama's orders earlier, we will now have to go through the Birkbeck file together so that you will at least have some idea of what you are talking about in Berundi."

"No problem, Tony, I can sleep during what I am led to believe is a pretty lengthy plane journey tomorrow."

***

The aircraft that Blake was directed to at a local private airfield the following morning appeared to be a single-engine Piper Cherokee, a make with which he was familiar but had never before flown in a model with the extra bulk, girth and wing thickness that this particular aeroplane displayed.

As he was ruminating upon this apparent anomaly, a chipper, athletic little man in his early middle years bounced down out of the cockpit and, having relieved him of his bag, grabbed his passenger by the hand. "You must be Richard Blake, great to see you. I am your pilot, Rupert Farris, eager and ready to fly to Quala in the Central African Republic, which is the nearest airstrip to where mysterious Berundi is situated. I trust that you have had a pee, etcetera, as it is a bloody long way and, wind permitting, will take us at least five hours. If you are all set, whilst I stow your bag, hop up on the wing and strap yourself into the seat next to mine in the front."

Feeling no match for this self-assured loquaciousness, as he was suffering from a mild hangover, Richard muttered a brief greeting and did as he was told; after which, within a few minutes, they were roaring down the runway and lifting off.

Once the plane was set on an even course, Rupert turned to his passenger and commented, "I noticed you studying my old bird with confused curiosity?"

Richard smiled as he nodded. "True indeed, because, having flown in this Piper model several times, I have never ever seen one this shape."

SIX

The reply was fascinating but logical. "Ah, well, she is built for purpose not for splendour, you see. I am very much of a one-man band and have now owned this baby for five years since I retired from the RAF. If you want to run a profitable aerial taxi business in this benighted part of the world, it is vital to minimise your exposure to the bribery, corruption and intimidation of the disadvantaged native population. This means that the need to refuel in remote areas has to be kept to a bare minimum. Thus, when I renovated this beauty after purchase, I not only jazzed up her engine speed from 120 to a maximum 155 miles per hour fully laden, but also, her fuel tanks were expanded to allow for a 1,200-mile single leap."

"I must say, Rupert, that's a big relief as I had anticipated us having to stop off somewhere in the bush during today's lengthy journey."

"No, sir, as I told you, five hours will do it and no stop-overs."

The flight then continued most pleasantly, with both parties reminiscing over their service careers, where ex-Wing-Commander Farris had actually diced with the Hun during the latter stages of World War II.

It was not until the pilot was about to commence his final descent that neo-disaster struck.

On glancing below in primary preparation for landing, Rupert excitedly ejaculated, "Fucking hell! Hang onto your nuts, Captain!" as he violently lurched the plane sideways and rolled her right over before dropping like a stone as what appeared to be a hurtling fireball narrowly missed them.

As Farris then steadied his machine back on course with considerable difficulty, he sweatily commented, "Let's get my 'wonderbird' down as soon as possible and prey to whatever gods we have left that there is not another one of those fireworks in the vicinity and offer supreme thanks that the one we managed to avoid was not a diligent heat-seeker. The wings only managed to endure my desperate manoeuvre because of their strengthening and the fact that we had already burnt a lot of the fuel. Also, a million thanks to you, RAF, for training me so well. Captain Blake, I hate to say so, but, as I am too old to make enemies anymore, it seems that someone out there really does not like you!"

With feigned bravado, Richard responded, "That may be, but, as I am now purely a boring businessman, I have no reason to suppose why. Also, because we were flying over virtually uninhabited semi-desert terrain, that missile must have been fired from a mobile launcher, so there is no possible chance of identifying its origin."

As they then landed on the primitive Quala airstrip, Rupert intoned, "I believe that we are both in desperate need of a drink, which I know that we can find in a corrugated iron shithouse of a bar near the police shack. I think it is also high time for us to have a brief heart-to-heart chat."

"Just so, Rupert. I am being met by a Berundi government chauffer, but he will have to cool his heels whilst we achieve these priorities."

So, whilst the agitated driver who had greeted him at the door of the plane on arrival fidgeted frustratedly in his highly buffed Buick, Richard and Rupert secured some barely drinkable, very warm beer.

SIX

In view of their recent incredibly close shave, the intrepid pilot then put forward a more than reasonable suggestion. "Listen, Dick, I want you to know that I found our short time together delightful and you are very much my kind of chap. Anyhow, now that I am reasonably settled down with an adorable Asian lady and the business is doing OK, I am not prepared to risk my arse for you, particularly as I suspect that you are up to something which has nothing to do with business. Hence, although I am being well paid to eventually get you back to Port Harcourt, there is no way that I am now prepared to fly you there personally."

Farris then opened an attaché case and withdrew a bundle of flight schedule brochures which he perused briefly. "I always have these with me in case I get stuck somewhere. You can contact me at the decidedly dodgy 'Quala Hotel Imperiale' when you are ready to depart. I shall then be more than happy to fly you to Bangui M'Poko Airport. The flight actually takes less than an hour, but as the controllers there are sometimes awkward over private landings, we should allow up to a couple of hours. From there, you can grab a South African Airways turbo-prop flight to Jos in Central Nigeria, where Nigerian Airways offers regular flights to Port Harcourt. The bad news is that there are only two Bangui/Jos flights a week, the next one being at 1530 hours tomorrow morning and, because of the timing, you will not be able to catch the second leg until the following day. Fair enough?"

Dick had only one possible answer. "Well, it will bloody well have to be and, as I can't drink any more of this gonorrhoeal camel's piss, let's finish off this decent scotch in my hip flask fairly sharply before my poor chauffeur suffers a nervous breakdown. Incidentally, on consideration, and for reasons that you may be able to guess, so far as your client, Fort Lamy and his gang are concerned, our skyrocket incident never occurred. When asked, I will say that the reason for altering my return flight arrangements was that I became unnerved by flying over mainly wilderness in a single-engine aircraft. Hopefully you will back this up, OK?"

Rupert nodded as he removed Richard's flask from his mouth. "That's absolutely fine, so long as you do not impugn my piloting skills."

During the subsequent hour-long limousine journey to Berundi, where the border access from the Central African Republic turned out to be but a sparsely guarded iron-grilled double gate, Blake had time to ruminate over the best course of action to take during his imminent encounter. One obvious conclusion he did arrive at was that to mention his recent missile drama would be totally counterproductive as it would create a large question mark over Birkbeck's security credibility.

On then passing through an arched entrance with artificial battlements, which was manned by black-uniformed armed guards, he was greeted at the foot of a red-brick stairway by a handsome, jet black man of his own age, wearing an immaculate, richly bemedaled khaki uniform of a full colonel.

"Birkbeck's Mr Blake, I presume. I trust that your long journey out was at least bearable. I am Albert Unegby and enjoy the dubious honour of being this humble little country's president. Although it is somewhat late, I thought we might extend my most promising discussions with your firm's Robert Steinbeck over lunch, when Zafia Kato – my CFO or, as you might call him, Chancellor of the Exchequer – will join us."

Politely chuckling at the presumed witticism, Blake confirmed his identity as they ascended the stairway and by the time they reached the glazed double doorway at the top had agreed upon a first-name relationship. Thence, two smartly attired, red-sashed corporals with side arms escorted them into a lavishly furnished dining room with bay windows overlooking an uncommonly verdant lawn.

Kato, which was all Albert Unegby saw fit to call him, turned out to be a dowdy and introverted contrast to his boss, with his hunched bearing and crumpled, stained white suit. Nevertheless, when a more than adequate meal, accompanied by suitable wines, was completed and papers were produced over the coffees, the accountant's doleful features brightened up as he entered his comfort zone and took matters over.

Richard, if he had not thoroughly studied his file, would have been totally out of his depth with this kind of bartering but, in less than an hour, a form of conclusion was reached after Unegby assumed control again in the final lap.

"So, Richard, without further ado, if all things are as they have been described, how much is your company prepared to invest in our patriotic project?"

Blake returned his intense stare. "Well, Albert, if we are reasonably confident that you have a good chance of achieving your aims, I suggest that three million pounds should fit the bill."

Without deferring to his superior, Kato scoffingly intoned, "Totally out of the question; any sum below five million pounds could not possibly earn Birkbeck the right to a significant share of oil when we eventually control supplies."

Obviously irritated by his sidekick's intrusiveness, Unegby cut back in, "Thank you for your input, Kato; you can now depart and leave me to stimulate our guest's generosity."

Then, following his boffin's departure, he strolled to a side table and poured two generous brandies, which he set down as he reseated himself at the table opposite Richard.

"Well, my friend, as so far you have only seen diagrams of our training facilities; in order to enhance your offer, I will amplify their quality by showing them to you personally right now. You will then see for yourself that, in addition to a substantial amassing of military equipment, we have already recruited a considerable number of volunteers for military training, with a great deal more men eagerly awaiting to join up. Please excuse me for a moment whist I pop out and make an urgent phone call before we leave."

When Richard was then conducted around the now largely completed base with an enthusiastic commentary by his host, he was indeed greatly impressed.

In addition to extensive barrack-room facilities and a well-stocked armoury, assault courses, gymnasia and hand grenade throwing pits were in evidence.

Also, in an area skirting the expansive parade ground zone was an eclectic array of heavier ballistic weaponry, some armoured cars and even a couple of tanks, plus a fully equipped four hundred-metre firing range.

However, with his practised soldier's eye, what did not quite ring true for Blake was that, in spite of the fair scattering of recruits, there appeared to be a dearth of African officers and NCO instructors.

Apart from this, although he was proudly shown around the recruits' impressive living quarters, Unegby assiduously avoided going near a smaller, but more stylishly appointed, centrally located building with its own forecourt.

Nevertheless, the invitee decided not to mention these observations and eventually accompanied his guide back to a conference room and got seated around a large writing table. "Well, how about it now, Richard? I am sure that tour must have slackened your purse strings?"

"I have to admit, Albert, that it was all pretty impressive and has persuaded me to suggest to my senior partner that we up our offer to your required five million pounds. In fact, as we communicate by code for politically sensitive deals like this one, I could use your telex right now, if I may, to contact him at our Port Harcourt office, as we travelled out to Africa together."

"If your messages are securely coded, Richard, I am delighted for you to use my machine, but who said that five million is necessarily sufficient?"

"Your exciting 'Chancellor'. I happen to be adept at reading body language, Albert."

"Shit, Richard, I shall have to send him on a severe crash course in diplomacy and dramatic art!"

Whilst deigning to display no amusement at this quip, Blake fielded a contentious question. "As a would-be investor, how much money are you making from your specialised slave business? I presume that this questionable operation is housed in the over-elaborately designed complex that we passed through en route to your military zone."

Unegby indulged in an unsavoury licentious leer. "Goodness me, you boys have done your homework. Actually, without wishing to overburden good old British hypocrisy, that additional venture is purely based upon our honing and producing sophisticated servants who chose to seek no financial reward. The males are all trained in at least one useful skill, whilst females receive a comprehensive course in obedient and versatile sexual expertise. During their time under instruction in the premises you so cleverly identified, all of them enjoy luxurious quarters. They also even have access to their own hospital, where sadly, some male contenders for certain Middle Eastern clients have to be painlessly afflicted with soprano voices. So far as the productivity of the venture is concerned, this potentially lucrative show is not as yet fully on the road. Nonetheless, even though it was originally conceived purely as a cover-up, with an option for males to sign up for military duties if they preferred to do so, we are now keen to progress the programme.

I must say that I would be both surprised and disappointed if this presented any moral problems for you guys. Especially as I have taken the liberty of booking you in with Nadia tonight, who is one of our most accomplished lady trainees. I am afraid that this will have to be in her quarters, for security reasons, but am certain that you will have no complaints. She will also prepare you some supper as I regret that I already have other plans for this evening, which unfortunately do not include the excesses that you will be enjoying."

Richard was well attuned to making pragmatic snap decisions and so his response primarily took into account the fact that Nadia's accommodation had to be located in close proximity to the mystery military building about which he needed to know more.

"Well, Albert, hypocrites us Brits may be, but gentlemen amongst us, such as I, have a sense of priority and strongly believe that the worst social crime of all is to turn ones back on a generous offer."

The president instantly burst into laughter. "I will take that as a yes, then. Good for you, old boy. Let me show you where our telex room is and then, after you have sent your coded message, you will be escorted to meet your date, in whose deluxe chamber your luggage is already stowed.

Lydia turned out to be a classically beautiful half-French twenty-year-old lady from Cameroon, whose curvaceous golden limbs were clad in a skimpy red silk mini dress, under which no undergarments were in evidence.

As she greeted Richard sweetly in her native French tongue, where Richard was fortunately fluent, he sensed that his resolve to avoid intimacy with an enslaved soul was already seriously waning.

Anyway, duty first and, avoiding the gaze of her slightly slanted dark green eyes, as she tantalisingly reclined on a couch, he firmly seated himself at a small, neatly laid dining table and demanded, "*Je veux le diner avant romance.*"

Having received a lingering, passionate kiss, his command was obeyed via her personally serving a typically French national dish of *biftec, pomme frits* and *petit pois*, followed by *fraises a la crème*, all accompanied by a bottle of basic, rich vin rouge.

On then avoiding the temptation of *café avec cognac*, Richard still opted to shelve what had now become his ultimate evil intent, in favour of dutifully carrying out the surveillance mission first.

"Sorry, *ma cherie*, but I left something most important behind and will return very soon."

Following another succulent embrace with the unfortunate girl, who had probably been ordered to retain his presence via sexually indulging him on pain of punishment, he departed and cautiously wended his way to the training base.

Fortune was not on Blake's side, however, because as he crept through the half-open metal-studded wooden gate of his targeted block, a guard appeared from nowhere, gripping a Lee-Enfield rifle which was pointed straight at him. As an attempt to draw his Beretta was likely to prove suicidal, in the urgent interests of self-preservation he shouted, "Hold your fire; I am a guest of Colonel Unegby's."

As a result of this caution, the confused soldier, who was probably a raw recruit, fired his particularly noisy

SIX

weapon into the air, which created an instant dramatic response.

With the dimmed pathway lights suddenly blazing, figures poured from the surrounding accommodation and the intruder was soon encircled by a hoard of uniformed oriental guards.

As Richard's recently healed body was being firmly gripped by his captors, a squat, ugly but authoritative individual of their ilk, whose jacket displayed the rank of colonel, approached him.

"I wish to know your reason for spying upon my team and, should you fail to provide me with a satisfactory reply, I shall painfully persuade you to cooperate. I am waiting!"

Whilst remaining mute and anticipating the worst, Blake was highly relieved when a breathless and obviously highly agitated Albert Unegby appeared on the scene.

"It is fine, Colonel Wing, this man is on our side, and I will take care of him. Please come to see me in my office, Shen, at 0900 hours tomorrow, when I will fully explain matters to you."

With that, Blake was released and ushered away but, as soon as they were out of earshot, Unegby royally reprimanded him. "What the fuck do you think you are up to? Do you have some sort of death wish? Spying upon our crème de la crème senior echelon, you bloody fool, why?"

As Richard was determined to take no more of this haranguing, he switched into an equally aggressive mode. "Because you were a bloody fool by deliberately avoiding that particular compound during my detailed tour earlier. And how dare you address me in such an overbearing manner? If you want my employer's investment, it will be subject to your instant apology for a start, and I shall now return to the lady who has proved to be the only civil human company that I have encountered this evening."

Unegby smiled smugly. "I am afraid that will not be possible as she is now in disgrace and will be under arrest for not reporting your departure. Naturally, the abode is still at your disposal and at least you might now get a good night's sleep. I suggest that we meet first thing tomorrow when we have all cooled down and, hopefully, you will have received a response to your earlier communication. I do apologise unreservedly, though, for my outburst, Richard. These are indeed trying times for all of us!"

Arriving in the main office building at 8am following a restless night, tainted with guilt over what horrors Lydia might have endured as a result of his actions, Blake retrieved the telex that had just arrived for his attention from Birkbeck's Port Harcourt office. Then, on being directed by a fawning female secretary to an anteroom, he put on a charade of decoding a load of gibberish.

This being completed, with a nod from a uniformed armed sentinel, he knocked and entered Unegby's flamboyantly furnished bureau, where, on his appearance, the colonel nimbly emerged from behind his gargantuan desk and shook his hand in eager greeting.

"A very good morning to you, Richard, and I trust that you enjoyed a good night's sleep, in spite of that unfortunate minor upheaval last night. You are refreshingly punctual at eight-forty, especially as I understand that you have now decoded your telexed response, which hopefully bears good news."

Feeling in no way inclined to mirror Unegby's exuberant bonhomie, Blake decided to adopt a tersely formal approach. "Good morning, President. I did, in fact, suffer a restless night and trust that young Lydia has not been abused for what you have chosen to regard as my indiscretion. The response from our Port Harcourt office is inconclusive but reasonably encouraging and I have been requested to return as soon as possible for further discussions, which will also have to include Guernsey executives. I have already phoned my pilot, who has been residing at a hotel in Quala and is now on his way to the aerodrome in order to refuel and meet me there at ten. As I am packed and ready to go, I would appreciate your supplying me with transport as soon as possible."

By the time Richard's stilted rhetoric was concluded, Unegby had reseated himself behind his desk with a far-from-friendly glint in his dark eyes.

"So, Mr Blake, I can only say that I am highly disappointed with your company's procrastination and, unless there is a more positive response within ten days, we shall search for additional finance elsewhere. I might also suggest that Birkbeck's next visitation should be undertaken by someone who, unlike you, has meaningful authority and at least a smattering of diplomatic skills. Your car will be at the foot of the steps outside in five minutes. Good day to you, sir."

As Blake descended the steps, with a corporal carrying his luggage, he was dwelling upon the fact that he had totally screwed up matters by revealing himself to be an agent provocateur.

However, had Blake been aware of the decision that was made at the meeting which followed his, he would have been infinitely more concerned.

Colonel Shen Wing was trembling with fury as he crashed the door of Unegby's office door wide open and stormed in. "What the fuck are you up to? Have you totally lost what little reason you ever possessed? I report to you, as requested, only to observe the subject of our intended discussion waltzing out scot-free."

Unegby was having an exceptionally bad day, and it was still barely 9am. "Come on, be reasonable, Shen, Blake happens to represent investment."

His vehement critic was not to be so easily pacified. "I don't give a shit if he has all the funds of the Bank of England at his disposal. You make me and my men hide whilst you show this bastard round, then after dark he breezes into our compound and, within minutes, learns of our existence anyway and, thanks to your addressing me by name, now has my specific identity. He must be eliminated as soon as possible and, if he is not, I shall seriously consider withdrawing my training team, which will mean that your main backer's regular and generous cash injection will cease to flow!"

As it was abundantly clear to the president that this officer, who played a key part in the grand scheme of events, was in no mood for argument, acquiescence was his only option.

"Well, hopefully Richard Blake, about whom you feel so strongly, is but a senior messenger. Fortunately, whilst

SIX

I had supposed that he was returning in the Cherokee that brought him out here, I have just been advised by our friends in Port Harcourt of his actual travel itinerary and for some reason, he is returning via the 1530 SAA flight from Bangui in the Central African Republic to Jos in Central Nigeria, where he plans to catch a Port Harcourt plane tomorrow. If we can manage to smuggle one of your subtle elimination artists onto his flight, our overzealous snooper could be discretely eliminated when he stays over at Jos airport."

Colonel Wing walked around the desk and slapped his now fellow conspirator on the back. "My other self… at last! The best man for the job is Chim Pui, who can snap a man's cervical vertebra by just winking at him."

"My God, Shen, your idioms are sometimes so typically British that they haunt me with memories of my earlier years of repression."

"Never mind all that nostalgic bullshit, sir. And I might add that, for this job, Chim is particularly well suited because, as he has a white mother, his appearance is Caucasian, so he is unlikely to set off any alarm bells with our intended victim. However, I shall need your executive jet later to get him to Bangui in good time. How the hell is Blake getting there?"

A far more relaxed Colonel Unegby responded, "He is most probably gearing up to getting under way shortly in his quaint mono-prop plane to which our driver is en route to deliver him at the Quala airstrip."

***

The day before Blake's fractious departure from Berundi, on checking his telex machine in the Port Harcourt Birkbeck office during the early evening, Price had been intrigued to find a very recent Jingles communication, where the decoded message read:

> *plotter someone attempted to shoot down my plane which do not tell anyone*
> *substantial military development here with expanding troop supply all impressive*
> *urgently send six-line coded reply by 7.30am tomorrow, content not important*
> *returning bangui jos tomorrow with you the day after on thursday pm*
> *full report when back including financial negotiation jingles*

On reading through his translation, Plotter muttered to himself, "Bloody hell, something must be leaking somewhere. Which bastard would have taken the pot shot and why?"

With that, a familiar voice from the unlocked door behind him chirped, "Do you know what they say about people who talk to themselves? So, what's up, big boy, and have you heard from Dick yet?"

"As a matter of fact, Cynthia, I just have, but there is nothing new to report, except that it seems he has decided to return via Bangui in the CAR and Jos, on regular airlines, probably because your lot only provided him with a meagre little kite – I don't blame him."

The young lady smiled sympathetically. "To be quite frank, Tony, neither do I. When is he due in?"

Swiftly stuffing the message transcript into his pocket, the major replied, "Sometime on Thursday, but to do so he is apparently having to leave Berundi tomorrow, which would suggest that his trip can hardly have been a roaring success. Anyway, I imagine you are here because you are joining the dinner at seven-thirty tonight in the Arthurian Club, to which General Okafor has kindly invited me."

"That's right, I thought that we might go along there together. Needless to say, Fort Lamy is seething with his customary insecure outrage over being left out."

For this comment, Price laughingly berated her. "Watch it, my girl, he happens to be your superior officer."

"Oh, sorry, Tony, I thought he was really only Dick's wayward platoon sergeant!"

Their dinner turned out to be a jolly event, very much illuminated by the host's inimitable humorous charm. Nevertheless, Price was fascinated to observe that much of the general's witty repartee masked a fair number of subtly posed sensitive questions.

As it was only 10.15pm when Okafor took his leave, Cynthia insisted on Price escorting her to the Hilton's Bon Nuit Salon for a nightcap and some dancing where – surprise, surprise – the discotheque had been closed for three months!

"That means that we will have to round off our perfect evening relaxing with some champagne in your room, my darling. I won't tell Dick if you promise not to as well," the dusky seductress then bargained.

At that moment, Tony experienced a fleeting sense of sympathy for the sexually berated friend whom he was supposed to be chaperoning.

After all, when a sweet-smelling, perfectly groomed beauty caresses your body with hers, what else is a fellow to do other than respond with alacrity? Thus, a breach of military protocol and an abandonment of moral principles instantly became the order of the night!

Waking up with a start the following morning, Price frantically studied his watch in the half-light and was relieved to make out that it was only 6.45am.

He had a telex to urgently send off by 7.30am and so preferred not to awaken his dereliction of duty who was snoring sweetly beside him.

With extreme stealth, the guilty philanderer, managed to disentangle himself, dress and be on his way to the Birkbeck office without arousing the serene *conquistadora*.

On his later arrival at HQ, feeling fatigued and grubby, the last thing that Price needed was to be semi-asphyxiated by Fort Lamy's halitosis as the petulant officer yelled in his face, "Listen to me, young man, I am sure that your orders from Colonel McCarthy clearly defined that I am your primary agent out here. How is it, then, that I appear to be getting information to which you are privy second hand? For a start, why the hell is Blake flying back via regular airlines when, for security reasons, I authorised the hiring of a perfectly adequate private aircraft for him to use?"

Tony controlled his irritation with difficulty, as he did feel slightly guilty over the fact that he tended to overlook the presence of this decidedly unattractive character.

SIX

"I am so sorry that you see things that way, sir, and will pay greater attention to keeping you fully in our somewhat obscure picture in the future. Hopefully, Blake will be able to fill us all in when he returns on Thursday afternoon."

The exasperated brigadier then made an extraordinarily ominous remark. "You two puppies should be far more cautious over the people that you do appear to be freely talking to!"

SEVEN

Following a jolly reunion with Rupert Farris as they flew from Quala to Bangui, Blake arrived at M'Poko Airport in a far more relaxed frame of mind than he had been in on his departure from Berundi. This was in spite of Rupert having been obliged to stooge for an hour whilst awaiting permission to land and the fact that he still had a lengthy wait before his Jos flight was due to depart.

Flight SAA 27, in a perceptibly weathered Vickers Viscount, took off only five minutes late, with an estimated flight time of two and a half hours. As the passenger complement was only half a dozen Africans and one other Westerner – in the form of an intense-looking skinny young man – cabin service was prompt; drinks were complimentary; and a marginally edible goulash-based meal was served en route.

To take his mind off the confusing imbroglio that the Berundi mission had become, Richard sat back with his champagne and mused upon his intriguing destination, which he had last visited for a rugby weekend in 1960.

SEVEN

Jos is situated on a central Nigerian plateau and, at four thousand feet above sea level, enjoys the largely sweltering country's most temperate environment.

In 1905, the early colonial Brits discovered vast sources of tin in the area, which rapidly transformed the formally obscure township into a thriving community. This situation then morphed into a financial bonanza when, in the early forties, columbite was also found to be abundantly available. This mineral was for a time the only viable agent for hardening steel sufficiently to tolerate the extreme heat generated by jet engines.

Unfortunately, when alternative sources were eventually discovered elsewhere, the Jos residents' opulent lifestyle imploded, and their luxurious metropolis deteriorated into a ghost town version of its former self.

It was only a short time after this debacle struck that Richard had last been a visitor so, as his plane came in to land, he tipsily vowed that, in the interests of mental recuperation, he would spend the inter-flight break in town. This would enable him to revisit Zimba's Palace, where he and his teammates had indulged in decadent revelry a decade earlier.

Meanwhile, Chim Pui, having conceived a straightforward airport hotel extermination strategy, was infuriated when, on clearing customs, his quarry hopped into a cab, which he was hurriedly obliged to follow.

Unfortunately, when Richard endeavoured to check into the taxi driver-selected Veranda Hotel, he was informed by a receptionist that, due to a victualler's convention, their only decent rooms were not available until 9.30pm.

Not to be discouraged, he decided to pursue his original nostalgic intent in the interim, even though, on making enquiries with Audu, the affable concierge, he was informed that the establishment he sought was now a 'café', rather than a 'palace'. Nevertheless, his advisor did reckon that the venue was still great value for a visit and only half an hour's walk away, for which directions were duly supplied.

As Richard felt he needed some fresh air, having secured his hand luggage and requested that a suitable room was held for him, he proceeded on foot into the moonlit winter evening. Moments later, his slender erstwhile travelling companion slipped out of the hotel's street bar door in hot pursuit.

Fifteen minutes into his short hike, Blake heard it again, as the back of his neck tingled with the awareness of lurking menace. One indistinct step-like sound in an ill-lit deserted street could be an animal; a second might be imagination but, as Blake had learnt through training and experience, a third one invariably signalled that he was being followed and probably in danger. A situation which, in view of recent events, needed to be ruthlessly addressed, but this was where the old soldier was to carelessly underestimate the guile of his pursuer.

Having rounded the next corner, he ducked into an ally on his left and waited with his back flat against a wall and the Beretta drawn and ready.

As with so many things in life, timing is of the essence and sadly, this equally applies to impending death. The would-be victim simply remained static for too long, thus awarding his stalker with that extra fraction of time in which to gain an advantage.

In a violent instant, Blake's legs were buckled and his gun gone as his head was smashed against the wall by the descent of a sinuous body from above him. Via his skills, Chim Pui had easily sussed out his victim's simple ploy and noiselessly clambered onto the roof of an adjacent bungalow.

What saved Blake from total disaster was the narrowness of the alley as, although it instantly became obvious that his diminutive aggressor possessed formidable unarmed combat skills, he had insufficient space in which to fully utilise them.

Nonetheless, the expertly applied pressures and blows that Pui was still able to inflict steadily wore Richard down, in spite of his superior stature, and soon rendered him flat on his back.

It was then that fortune decided to smile upon Captain Jingles for the first time in almost two disastrous days. As he desperately grappled with a knife-bearing arm, his thigh came into contact with what had to be his pistol. Taking the chance of momentarily disengaging his right hand from Chim Pui's steadily descending forearm, Blake grabbed the Beretta by the barrel and smashed the butt into the larynx of his assailant, who instantly went limp and silently rolled off him.

It then took several minutes for Blake to recover his composure and establish that the dangerous little athlete was as dead as a doornail. What to now do with the body?

Most conveniently, an instant solution was but a few yards away.

The small house that the attacker had jumped from was little more than a rotting, deserted shack but, as was revealed on pulling open a side gate, in the back yard there was a well with a flat stone across the top of it. Utilising what little energy he had left, Richard managed to drag the stone aside and dump Pui's body down the deep shaft before replacing it.

The victor then pocketed his late combatant's sequestered wallet and papers before wisely deciding to abandon the Zimba's Café outing and stiffly making his way back to the Veranda Hotel.

On arrival, the only member of the staff who was present in the reception area was Audu, the jovial Hausa concierge, who concernedly remarked, "That did not take long. What on earth happened to you, sir; did they throw you out?"

"Something like that, but I am absolutely fine. That is so long as you can check me in and let me use your telex machine immediately."

The concierge feigned perplexity. "Well, sir, I will check you in but am afraid that you cannot access the room for another hour. Also, as the office closes at seven and it is now nine, so far as using the telex is—"

A twenty-dollar bill swiftly hit the jackpot, which was probably far more than the poor fellow's weekly wage.

However, when the now beaming custodian was recording the generous hotel guest's details and checking his passport, he did remark, "Well, Mr Soreiro, I would never have guessed that you were an American."

SEVEN

To which the reply was, "Living in San Francisco refined my Texan accent."

***

At 8am the following morning, Plotter decoded his incoming Jingles telex from the night before with increasing incredulity:

> *plotter unegby not happy with me and being kept partly in dark by his own side*
> *got caught spying on large oriental training force c o colonel wing*
> *details my amended route back obviously blown by someone*
> *big attempt my assassination Jos this evening*
> *obliged to kill assassin chim pui hk chinese not peoples republic*
> *as his body hidden believe I should fake dead*
> *flying harcourt as planned but using usa alias*
> *meet me alone secretly for full update beware being followed*
> *advise by return airport meeting place timing to fit landing number na four three two jingles*

This extraordinary news raised so many open questions that Tony wisely decided not to indulge in fretful second guessing and wait until he saw Jingles before making any ongoing decisions.

Having then telexed his now dearly departed friend

to meet him at the Boot and Flogger Pub opposite airport departures, he shredded all relevant papers. Whilst doing so, he experienced more than a twinge of guilt over losing the translation of Richard's last message, especially as he had a nagging suspicion over who may well have procured the transcript!

In view of his perplexed frame of mind, the only positive act that Plotter then performed before heading off to the airport was one of tactical diplomacy when, on passing through HQ, he took Fort Lamy aside.

"Listen, sir, I am truly sorry that you appear to be taking offence over being left out of the loop when you are, in all fairness, Colonel McCarthy's nominated contact. Thus, on Blake's return, I believe the three of us should got together for a proper down-to-earth conversation."

The *d'habitude* patronising, but once again possibly portentous, response was, "Good for you – maybe you are beginning to see some sense at last, my boy!"

Then, as he was departing from the office, Tony was button-holed by Cynthia at the doorway who whispered, "Are we going to see each other tonight, then?"

"Well, my sweet, as Blake is due to turn up sometime this afternoon, that may prove a little difficult as he will probably have a great deal to report. Apart from which, I am supposed to be his chaperone!"

The urgent murmured reply was, "Well, that's fine, but as his superior officer, you should not allow him to deter you from fulfilling your lustful duties!"

Jingles was already in the designated rendezvous, nursing a beer, when Plotter arrived and, having bought two more foaming tankards, sat down opposite him. "I suppose that I really should have plonked a wreath on the table."

Richard visibly blanched. "Do not joke about it, there's a good chap; it was a near-run thing. My attacker really was a seriously able martial arts expert with neo-Olympic skills."

Price allowed himself a sarcastic snicker. "You are such a drama queen, Dick. He can't have been that good or you wouldn't be sitting here now! I do have to admit, though, you do have a mega 'shiner' blooming there."

"You should see it from this side, unsympathetic bastard. My body is literally black and blue all over. Anyhow, as I told you in my telex, to make my sudden disappearance watertight, I am now a Yankee. I have to say, though, that I never envisaged the so far unused American alias Falcon thrust upon me becoming used in Africa, but it has now turned out to be a godsend. Say hullo to Mr Tommy Soreiro!"

Major Price assumed an appropriately serious countenance as he produced a pencil and notebook from his jacket pocket. "Well, Jingles, as you have now selfishly died and left me to carry the torch alone, you had better put me fully in the picture concerning your adventures during the last forty-eight hours."

Having then fully outlined all the relevant events, dramas and disasters which had occurred during this time period, Captain Blake summarised his findings.

"The most maddening thing about our current Nigerian scenario is that nothing really quite fits and there are far too many 'unknowns' at present. However, I have gained the distinct impression that the other side has a surplus of cooks in their broth too, who are not all swimming in the same direction, and it is blatantly clear that the Port Harcourt HQ's security leaks like a bloody sieve. For a start, whilst we are aware of the individuals who knew about my method of travel to Berundi, we do not have a clue who organised my fire-rocket reception. Nonetheless, I am ninety percent certain that Unegby was in no way aware of it and strongly of the opinion that, in apparent contradiction with certain other participants in his cartel, he genuinely believes that the Birkbeck potential investment is bona fide. This would indicate that the slime ball of a president is most probably only being tolerated because he is little more than a convenient frontman. Conversely, though, as I told nobody in Berundi about my amended flight arrangements, how come Mr Chim Pui was waiting for me in Jos, ready, willing and almost able to bump me off?"

At this point, Major Price somewhat ruefully cut in, "Possibly guilty as charged. I divulged this information to General Okafor and Cynthia over dinner on Tuesday evening. Poor old Fort Lamy was then very pissed off when he was only made aware of your travel plans via a third party the following day. He is, I am afraid, becoming extremely neurotic over our side-lining him in spite of his being the official MI6 local man. I have to say that, thanks in no small part to your negative input, we may have misjudged him."

"Maybe, Tony, but at least your innocent indiscretion has rooted out a couple of probable suspects, as did my

SEVEN

abortive probe into the mystery Barrack block which confirmed Berundi's reliance upon oriental military experts to train their troops. I believe there is distinct possibility that Colonel Shen Wing and his mob are really running the show in collaboration with the clandestine Nigerian bad boys over here. As my vanquished assassin turned out to be Hong Kong Chinese, there is a daunting possibility that the operation's military and financial support has nothing to do with the People's Republic at all and could be sitting on the UK's doorstep. To raise the exorbitant sums of money needed for launching a venture of this nature, the most likely alternative oriental source has got to be Hong Kong. If so, the revolution could end up as being internationally perceived to be a form of British colonial interference with the status of a free African country. That would certainly get old Falcon's bowels working overtime!"

Plotter took a long, contemplative draught of his beer.

"Although I am tempted to accuse you of wandering off into the realms of fantasy and being a 'drama queen' again, Jingles, your last suggestion does contain a daunting degree of possibility. I fully acknowledge the urgent need for the matter to be thoroughly checked out, but right now, Captain, we should focus upon immediate actions. For a start, you must get back to London post-haste via the first available flight, whilst obviously maintaining your US identity. On arrival, you should have no problem with securing a prompt audience with 'His Nibs', who will be gagging to see you, and during your jolly chat, please do mention your Hong Kong theory, with my blessing, if you have got the guts!

Meanwhile, I shall return to HQ and report your non-arrival, whilst emphasising that, on checking with Nigerian Airways, they told me that you were at no time registered as a passenger on their flight NA 432 from Jos today. Following orders from Falcon, I have to urgently undertake a Birkbeck revisit to Berundi to confirm their agreement in principal to making a five-million-pound investment and endeavour to ferret out as much additional info as I can whilst I am there."

Jingles frowned and stirred uneasily. "Taking into account how very uncordial my entente turned out to be, I consider that to be an unnecessarily dangerous course for you to steer, Major. Nevertheless, if you are reluctant to defy the führer and determined to risk your neck, do at least fly out via the Nigerian Airways tri-weekly direct flight to Bangui and arrange to be picked up there by Unegby's Lair Jet. Also, whilst you are making this precarious visit, beware of Colonel Wing big time as what little I saw of him convinced me that he is a ruthless thug who would stop at nothing to gain his ends. Anyway, your good news now is that you will no longer have to compete with me for Cynthia's favours... hey, wait a minute! It is patently obvious via your shifty expression that I have come second in the race already, you randy old hypocrite!"

At this, the stalwarts stood up and embraced. "No comment on your last uncalled for remark, Jingles. Just take care of yourself, my dear friend."

The simple reply was, "You too, Tony."

Once he was back at the HQ office, to avoid further insecure paranoia, Price immediately advised Hassan Fort

SEVEN

Lamy of Blake's disappearance, whilst omitting to make him aware of the true position. He adopted this course not only because of lingering doubts, but also as a form of test as, if Falcon had true faith in the brigadier, he would put him in the picture anyway.

Predictably, their meeting in the privacy of a conference room turned out to be a theatrical affair. "What do you mean Blake seems to have disappeared in Jos?" was petulantly demanded.

"Well, sir, there was no sign of him at the airport earlier and Nigerian Airways categorically denied that he was ever booked on their flight NA 432. However, when I checked with the South African Airways desk, they did confirm that he had flown from Bangui to Jos on their 1530 hours Viscount flight yesterday. The whole situation is a bloody mystery, particularly as I checked my Birkbeck office telex on the way here and Blake has not messaged me, which he would normally have done in the event of a change of plans."

"Well, Price, I do not know what you expect me to do about it but, as you two are such close buddies, I am amazed that you appear to be so relaxed over what could be a fatal situation." was Fort Lamy's suspicious response.

The time had now come for Plotter to fake losing his patience. "Listen, Brigadier, my relationship with Blake has always been purely professional and he is extremely capable of taking care of himself. As I am under orders to carry out a follow-up visit to Berundi, I shall now return to the Birkbeck office and continue to monitor the telex whilst arranging a direct regular airline fight to Bangui for myself as soon as possible. Thence, I shall telephone President Unegby to advise him of my imminent arrival and hitch a lift from Bangui to Berundi on his Lair Jet. Meanwhile, sir, as you are dying to become more involved, I suggest that you report Blake's apparent disappearance to your MI6 contacts in London and advise key members of the staff here, not least of all, General Okafor. In the meantime, I will let you know the timing of my proposed Berundi trip and keep you posted if I hear anything from Blake."

Having then departed from the conference room, leaving a somewhat bemused Fort Lamy gaping into his notebook, Tony murmured to Cynthia on his way out, "All clear; see you in the Hilton bar at seven-thirty, and book us a table at your favourite restaurant."

EIGHT

Having suffered a tedious convoluted journey from Port Harcourt, via Bahrain and Frankfurt, Richard did not arrive in London until Saturday morning. Then, having taken a black cab from Heathrow, he checked into the Eden Plaza Hotel just in time for a slap-up lunch, after which he indulged in a much-needed extended siesta.

By 7.30pm he felt sufficiently revitalised to call Falcon, for which in view of the late weekend hour, he used the 'express emergency' line from the hotel bar's public telephone, which instantly triggered a severe reprimand.

"So, Jingles, why are you using this number, which had better be from a call box?"

"Checking in, as I just arrived back from Nigeria in my coffin." A badly timed jest!

"Checking in? Checking in, Jingles? Unlike your last call via this exclusive route, which was certainly verging on an express emergency, you now have the effrontery to use this line for a virtually social call, how dare you? I wish you were in a bloody coffin! Anyhow, as you are now at least in touch, having obviously taken some form of scenic route home, I expect to see you at the MI6 building at 0900 hours on Monday morning. On your arrival, give your first name only to the front desk and you will be escorted to my office." The phone then went dead.

The next call that Richard made was from his room and inspired an infinitely friendlier reaction, once he had penetrated a barrier of fawning servants. "Toby, I trust that you are in great shape, as ever?"

"Richard, my dear fellow, I am in top form; how the hell are you? Apart from being your close friend, I also happen to be your boss – where the hell are you?"

"Well, Toby, I have been wondering that myself over the past week or so, but right now I have just arrived back in London and was hoping that we might touch base. However, on phoning your Cheyne Walk abode, I was told that you are spending the weekend down there at your country pile."

"I have actually been in Redstone Manor for the whole week with Elsa and two of my girls, preparing for rapidly approaching Christmas, you old Scrooge. But this does not prevent us from getting together, Dick. As it is a bit late this evening and you have been travelling, come out to Farnham on the ten o'clock train from Waterloo tomorrow morning. I will have you picked up from the station and then you can stay here and ride back to London with me on Monday. Elsa, Loraine and Liz would love to see you; also it is high time for the two of us to discuss one or two boringly serious matters."

EIGHT

"Toby, I am delighted to accept your kind offer but regret that, as I have an urgent appointment with one Colonel Ignatius McCarthy in Westminster at nine on Monday, I shall have to minicab it back from Redstone before your bedtime tomorrow."

"If you have to see that hubristic bloody clockwork soldier, fair enough. However, as I would not be seen dead with a minicab anywhere near my estate, the invitation is dependent upon Buster driving you home in the Bentley tomorrow evening."

"Game on, Toby, I look forward to seeing you and the girls for pre-lunch drinks tomorrow. Adieu until then."

Richard was mildly relieved that, out of his host's five daughters, only the two elder and more attractive ones would be present, but he was more than a trifle bemused to learn that his friend seemed to know Falcon. There was undoubtedly much to be revealed on the morrow!

The sojourn at Wellington-Green's magnificent Surrey home was a true delight, with his teenage daughters already displaying the wayward flirtatiousness to which their mother had been prone before Toby parked her in an extremely expensive siding. As so often happens, her replacement, Norwegian Eva, followed a similar pattern but with far more charisma and devoid of her predecessor's insufferable snobbery.

As forewarned, following a delicious traditional roast beef lunch, Richard's ebullient host suggested that they both withdraw to his study for cigars and brandies for a more solemn tête-à-tête.

As per his normal form, Toby swiftly got down to brass tacks. "So, Dick, via input at my neighbour, Rupert Muswell's dinner party last week, I gathered that you recently abandoned your convalescence in New York in order to take part in a vital Nigerian operation, from whence you have most probably just returned. It so happened that the chap who has now managed to partly bugger up our weekend, Colonel McCarthy, was also in attendance and, although he has about as much charisma as a camel's fart, he was full of praise for you. Naturally, even a patent bully boy like him was politely diplomatic in front of his boss, the home secretary. Nevertheless, he made it very clear to me that, as you have now become an important cog in his secret engine, being employed as a Lloyd's broker cannot be allowed to obstruct your patriotic duties anymore.

I realise that my providing you with an upfront cover may be necessary from time to time, and there is no way that I would dream of requesting your resignation.

Nonetheless, I have a business to run, and some of our co-directors are becoming a pain in the arse over your repeated lengthy absences. I therefore suggest that you forego your salary and remain on the board with an annual twenty-five percent commission entitlement for any business that you manage to produce. I am certain that this arrangement will be acceptable to the Board and, let's face it, on this basis Mark Lines alone should clock up at least $125,000 for you, and your Troll accounts are already worth around thirty thousand pounds. With your imminent MI6 salary and current army pension, you could end up

EIGHT

even wealthier than me, you presumptuous bastard! Also, remaining on my board of directors will maintain your 'working name' status, where you will be receiving your fist annual profit cheque in a couple of years' time."

"Toby, your proposal could not be more generous; I am heartily grateful to you for putting up with me until now and am delighted to accept your offer. However, as we are sort of talking shop, may I be a bore and ask you a shipping-related question?"

Richard's host refilled both their balloon glasses. "Fire ahead, young man, by all means, so long as the input that you require does not involve anything too technical."

"The Egyptian blocking of the Suez Canal almost four years ago, which created the need for larger tankers in order to cope with the vastly extended Europe/Arabian Gulf voyages, would appear to now be permanent. This seems to have created a situation where tanker owners, particularly those with what are known as 'super tankers' or VLCCs, are making a bloody fortune, of which I became particularly aware during my brief time broking for you. In fact, I recall my colleagues and I seriously struggling to complete the coverage of vast hull and consequential loss insurance amounts for Peter Smedvig's new 240,000-deadweight-ton vessel, 'VENI'. Your broking company appears to mainly deal with Norwegian, Swedish and Greek outfits, such as Lexton and Remos, but my big question for you is, are Far Eastern shipping companies doing equally well, particularly in Hong Kong?"

Toby allowed himself a chuckle. "My God, Dick, you are becoming a bore; I don't remember you stringing

117

together so many serious words ever before! But yes, you are right; nobody has ever seen such a shipping bonanza – in fact, Homar Lexton was telling me at one of his launch celebrations quite recently that, with freight rates where they are, three or four Europe/Gulf voyages can pay for a new ship. Unfortunately, we are not particularly active in the Far East as yet, but there certainly are numerous ship owners, mainly based in the Hong Kong vicinity, who are absolutely coining it. Also, these are not all mega operations, like CY Pew and YK Tang, as there are a number of highly profitable newer ventures, which operate in and around the same area."

Blake was obviously very pleased with this response. "Toby, that is precisely what I needed to know; thanks a million! As I have now completed my bout of tediousness and should not depart too late in order to be on reasonable form for my confrontation with 'Bollockly Bill' tomorrow, perhaps we should rejoin the ladies. Before we do, however, I must confess to being overawed by your ability to create unbelievably lasting impressions!"

"I am not getting your drift, Dick."

"In that case, I shall fully reveal my drift. There I am four and a half thousand miles away, having dinner with my friend Tony Price and a highly sexy, truly delightful local lady when, guess whose virtues she extols? How many Cynthias have you known during your wayward life?"

The accused beamed with a lascivious glint in his eye. "As she was Nigerian and no questions are indiscreet, only the answers, I have to identify her as a delicious

EIGHT

'Murray in a hurry' girl, but what the hell is she doing back in Africa?"

"A story too long to impart now but, as I told her that we were friends, she did send you fond loving salutations and still treasures your card for many happy memories it evokes!"

Toby was staring apprehensively at the closed door as he softly muttered, "In that case, Dick, as Eva is off on one of her Scandinavian jaunts on Tuesday, and you could be whisked away on a suicide mission at any time, let's get together at seven in the usual place on Wednesday and you can fill me in properly before going on the town."

"Great idea, sir, I could do with a London night out. Now, in the hope that we have had no eavesdroppers, we really should refrain from depriving the females of our company any longer."

***

Jingle's meeting with Falcon at his MI6 office the following morning unexpectedly turned out to be somewhat of a non-event.

Following a verbal Berundi visit report, where the prime reaction was criticism for not having yet committed it to writing, Falcon's mood became morosely contemplative.

In view of the fact that the Richard now had the wind in his tail in concerning the best way to move forward, he found the uncharacteristic negativity being displayed by his boss most frustrating.

"So, Jingles, how is my least favourite corpse, whose virtual death I consider to be an ill-conceived and unnecessary subterfuge. Do not respond to that! From what you have just told me, and from Plotter's last report, it would appear that you did not cover yourself with glory during your Berundi visit. What you do appear to have done, though, is recruit the major's support for this irritating Hong Kong theory of yours, which is becoming yet another thorn in my side. Bloody Colonial office, they were supposed to have routinely checked out this remote possibility but, since us losing the empire, their grossly overstaffed operation produces little more than pettifogging quibbles. I can, of course, overrule them, but I would prefer to review Plotter's findings, following his imminent visit to Berundi, before so doing—"

Blake just had to butt in before he exploded, "Hang on a moment, sir, I personally encountered Shen Wing and his clandestine echelon of military experts. Not only did they display greater sophistication and less subservience than any People's Republic soldiery that I have so far encountered, but also I have a theory concerning the source of their—"

"Silence, Jingles; you are here to listen, not to enlarge upon your unfounded theories, which are most probably emotionally accentuated by the fact that the assassin who endeavoured to slaughter you happened to be Hong Kong Chinese. Our cardinal problem currently is security on the ground in Port Harcourt which, as your own experiences bore out, appears to be non-existent, and so far, we have not got a clue what or where the source of the leaks might be.

EIGHT

Due to what we pay him alone, I have no doubts over the trustworthiness of Brigadier Fort Lamy. Also, my contacts in President Gowan's government will not hear a word said against Major General Okafor, over whom both you and Plotter now seem to have doubts. Nevertheless, as there are twenty-nine officers and other ranks working in that department, I have secured an unofficial undertaking from the Nigerian war minister that a discrete probe will now be carried out. The most frustrating aspect of the whole matter is that the key supporters of Gowan's virtual dictatorship are highly sceptical over our forebodings as they blindly believe that his newly reformed regime is unassailable.

All that being said, as I assume that you are now about to relinquish your career with Wellington-Green, to whom I have already spoken, you can consider yourself to be on temporary standby as a full-time employee of MI6. For this, you will obviously receive remuneration, which will commence from the first day of this month based upon a regular army captain's pay, plus reimbursements of any service-related expenses.

"I now intend to await Plotter the next report from Plotter, who I believe is off to Berundi today, and also input from the Colonial Office concerning Hong Kong, before deciding upon the best way to move forward. Meanwhile, so far as your personal situation is concerned, we are not prepared to fund hotel accommodation anymore so, bad memories permitting, your best course must be to move back into your totally renovated Tedworth square maisonette. As, for obvious reasons, a damage survey was out of the question, your insurers were surprisingly generous, and the leaseholders have now installed a sophisticated burglar alarm system. Full details on this front are with my ADC. Whatever you decide to do, make sure that we are aware of your home telephone number at all times and ring in here every day at 0900 hours. Is all that clear or do you have any questions?"

"As we appear to be very much between wind and water at present, no questions, Falcon, and thank you for sorting out my apartment."

***

Plotter opted to follow Jingles' advice and took a Nigerian Airways direct flight from Port Harcourt to Bangui at 8am on Tuesday. As this was in a Boeing 707 and Unegby had arranged for him to be picked up by his Lair jet, he reckoned on arriving at his mystery destination by 1pm.

Not least of all because there had been two attempts to eliminate Jingles during his recent visit, he was very aware that this was performing an extremely high-risk mission.

Also, his apprehensions had been in no way diminished by Cynthia's conduct when, following a night of particularly wild urgent passion, she had insisted on seeing him off.

Having tearfully pleaded with him to abort the project all the way to the airport, in her escalating pattern of desperation, she then had to be restrained by flight attendants when she clung onto him as he was passing through his departure gate.

EIGHT

Nonetheless, Plotter did not choose to believe that the young lady's desperation was in any way due to her awareness of sinister factors unbeknown to him.

Anyway, Price's concerns did not interfere with his patching up of a virtually sleepless night via taking deep naps on both of his flights.

However, when he was eventually dropped off at the Berundi base's red-brick main building, his mode of reception was nothing like the warm greeting that he understood Jingles had received.

Having been obliged to carry his luggage up a steep flight of brick stairs, a stern-faced Corporal then beckoned him through some double doors and lead him along a corridor to a cramped, windowless bedroom where tea and some sandwiches and were laid out on a small table.

Whilst Plotter was unpacking, little did he know that an intense conversation concerning his fate was taking place but fifty metres away.

Colonel Wing was being particularly aggressive as he addressed the president in his office. "Unegby, I do not give a shit about your naive belief that you can still squeeze some money out of this Birkbeck outfit, but if you now fail with the presumably more senior arsehole who just arrived, I shall be taking over. Fuck me, I am no businessman but, as their last guy is now missing and possibly dead, I am certain that any normal commercial outfit would have automatically thrown the towel in. The very fact that Birkbeck are still pursuing matters indicates to me that their operation is far more geared to snooping than investment."

The president was looking unpresidentially uncomfortable over these negative remarks from his key military advisor, who had become increasingly belligerent of late.

"OK, Shen, point taken, and I will ascertain what Mr Price's formal intentions are for making this visit when I meet with him very shortly. I might emphasise, though, that no one from the Birkbeck organisation has advised me that Blake has disappeared. Anyway, I can cover that point during my forthcoming meeting—"

Wing abruptly cut in, "For a start, it will be 'our' forthcoming meeting, as I intend to be present, and you are forbidden to make any reference whatsoever to Blake's vanishing. So far as that is concerned, I am monitoring, via a bribed airport official, all past and present passengers on flights out of Jos, with no results so far. Unfortunately, the railways are uncheckable. I insist that we are not in any way going to further complicate the issue with this man Price today. Simply bring him in here and get some money out of him before I am obliged to take far sterner measures."

Plotter had just half-heartedly consumed his dried-up spartan lunch when, following some shouting and stamping in the corridor, the corporal, who appeared to have been on guard, escorted him to a nearby reception area.

After a ten-minute wait, he was then ushered into a spacious, opulent office by a crisply uniformed female lieutenant, where he was confronted with the two men about whom he had heard so many bad things!

EIGHT

Whilst the oriental colonel remained seated in morose silence behind a massive mahogany desk, the flamboyantly uniformed and bemedaled African stood up and advanced to greet him.

"Mr Price, I presume. I am Colonel Unegby, President of Berundi, and this is my Military Chief of Staff, Colonel Wing. I trust you had a pleasant flight to Bangui and that our executive jet staff took good care of you.'

A brief, pleasantly banal conversation then ensued, during which Wing continued to remain silent until matters got down to brass tacks, thanks to Flotter opening the batting.

"Now then, gentlemen, I have had a chance to discuss the proposal put forward by my assistant Blake last week. So long as you are still eager to launch a naval back-up assault via chartered Congolese landing craft from Matadi port, the five million pounds is as good as yours."

At this, the oriental colonel blanched as he uttered his opening remark. "I am amazed that you saw fit to mention that remote operational aspect, Unegby, as it continues to be extremely politically sensitive with the Congolese."

The president then turned to his colleague, looking equally taken aback. "This must have been thrown into the negotiations by our CFO Zafia Cato when Blake was endeavouring to offer an unacceptable three million pounds."

In fact, Plotter had just scored by grossly exaggerating this obscure operational aspect, which Jingles had only fleetingly mentioned during his debriefing as a remote logical possibility. Fielding this as a supposition had now obviously created a reasonable excuse for the continued filibustering of a firm commitment!

"Well, gentlemen, in spite of the marine aspect obviously now being in doubt, so long as my opinion of your base's facilities echoes Blake's highly favourable findings, I am pretty sure that the other directors will still be fine with the offer. However, I must check this out with them in our London office and, if you avail me of your telex facility to send a message, in code of course, I will do so right now. After which, I would very much appreciate an escorted tour of your military base."

Wing abruptly rose to his feet with his fists clenched in an obvious fit of pique. "This had better be the last of your outfit's procrastinations, for your own good. Regardless of the president, I have decided that you are not leaving Berundi until your company's five million pounds is drafted to and cleared by the Berundi National Bank, the details of which, I understand you already have. As it is still early afternoon in London, that should be achievable today.

When you have messaged your people and hopefully received a satisfactory reply by return, I will arrange for you to be shown round our sophisticated complex by a sergeant major who, like me, is a Chinese-born Congolese."

> *falcon have invented assumption of a sea-born back-up force as a stalling tactic*
> *wing reacted badly and being very hostile*
> *he wishes hold me prisoner until sterling five mil cleared by Berundi nat bank*

EIGHT

important you send some form of reply by instant return plotter

After Price had been escorted out of the office to code and send this message, it was Unegby's turn to have a more contained moment of fury. "Listen, Shen, all you have now managed to achieve with that gentleman is to alienate him and probably the whole Birkbeck organisation as well. It is now highly likely when a reply arrives to his telex that our payment will not be considered until his safe return to Port Harcourt."

"I agree with you, Mr President, and maybe before that inevitable response is received, your precious Mr Price's goose will be cooked with me as the chef and you will keep your nose well and truly out of the broth of his imminent misfortune.

Listen, Albert, our key collaborators in Nigeria, with whom I enjoy a closer relationship than you do, have not fully kept you in the picture. We now know without doubt that, although Birkbeck is a bona fide oil company, they have been set up, probably by MI6, as a spying probe. When funds for our operation were tight, your insistence on pursuing this investment opportunity was agreed by a Nigerian majority, in total contradiction of my opinion. It then transpired that there were several other dissenters on my side, one of whom actually attempted a missile strike on Blake's incoming aircraft last week, which is undoubtedly why he altered his return routing. Let's face it, if you thought beyond the end of your nose, the deal you are so keen on could easily have been negotiated remotely and backed up photographically so far as the barracks' configuration and equipment are concerned. Anyhow, now that funds are flowing copiously from the Far Eastern ventures that supplied you with my training group, the unlikely possibility of an investment from Birkbeck is now a total irrelevance."

Unegby sat down resignedly behind his mammoth desk again. "If that is the case, OK, Shen, you win. However, I trust that I have not been kept in the dark as a result of any doubts over my total loyalty and devotion to the cause."

"My dear, Albert, there is no question of that; trust me!"

As the female lieutenant knocked on the door and announced the arrival of Wing's sergeant major, the president was not only facing up to the fact of who was really in charge but also how secure 'trust' in a man of Wing's evil character might prove to be.

Having stepped outside the office to give his tour guide a briefing, the Chinese colonel returned just as Price arrived to report on his exchange of messages, where the actual response had been:

plotter all facts noted but obviously no question of funds being paid
use your initiative to escape situation falcon

"OK, gentlemen, I received an immediate reply to the effect that the investment will be instantly transferred upon my safe return to Port Harcourt."

Wing responded in a tone which verged on friendliness. "The president and I will discuss that option

EIGHT

whilst you are enjoying your guided tour. For this, kindly join your escort, CSM Kelechi Jengo, who is waiting for you outside in reception."

After Plotter had departed, a now smiling Shen remarked to his newest best friend, "Albert, that is the last that you will ever see of that sneaky sleuth and no questions asked, if you please."

Whether or not it was a language barrier was not clear, but en route to their destination, Plotter's guide uttered not one word as he indicated the way with his pace stick.

Having skirted through what appeared to be the slave academy into what was obviously a military zone, it became immediately apparent that the majority of the instructors were oriental officers and NCOs.

Then, as they were passing a more compact and sophisticated barrack block, the silent escort suddenly drew his Colt 44 pistol and nudged Price into a guard house just inside its main gates, before roughly shoving him into a barred cell.

Having subjected him to a rigorous body search with the aid of an African corporal, during which his wallet and Pieper 7.65 sidearm were removed, Jengo handcuffed Plotter to an iron stanchion, before slamming and securing the cell door on his departure.

An hour then passed before the prisoner's most expected, but least welcome, visitor appeared, together with the sergeant major, who was now carrying a terrifyingly threatening object.

"So, Mr Price, the moment of truth has arrived for a friendly chat, during which I may ask you one or two leading questions," was Wing's opening remark as he settled on an adjacent wooden bench. "Although your Birkbeck masquerade may have fooled the president, via my being privy to a broader spectrum of information, I was never taken in. What is more, I am as sure that we will never see the five million pounds and certain that, like your colleague Blake, you are nothing more than a contemptable spy, who is undeserving of any humane empathy. Nevertheless, as it is rather hot and stuffy in here, I suggest that for your own comfort, you remove your clothing. Meanwhile, CSM, after you have unshackled our guest and assisted him to disrobe, why not then light the heater just in case he then becomes a trifle chilly."

At this point, the prisoner's main concern was to avoid the humiliation of losing control of his bowels when, after having had his clothes ripped off and been rehandcuffed, the warrant officer ignited his blowtorch.

"Now then, Price, for a start, I wish to know what happened to my expert assassin, Chim Pui and also what Blake's status is, otherwise we may be obliged to warm you up a little."

The fear of excruciating agony understandably now took over.

"Very simple, Wing, your hitman was no match for Blake, who killed him in self-defence, before leaving Jos by rail and eventually returning to London."

Affronted to hear in such a casual way that someone he considered to be the best had been outmanoeuvred, the colonel barely managed to remain calm. "Then I would be

EIGHT

right to assume that both you and Blake are trained and skilled MI6 agents?"

"That is correct."

"You can extinguish that flame, Sergeant Major. I happen to be familiar with the strong rumour which maintains that some years ago, a bogus mercenary, one Lieutenant Anthony Price, was burnt to death after being captured by Congolese soldiers during the Katanga conflicts. As we would not wish to simulate alleged African barbarism, I have devised a far more appropriate and fitting end for you. Appropriate, because its method was made possible by Mr Blake's nosiness, and fitting because it will truly test the MI6 unarmed combat skills that slew my key exterminator."

Price's relief over the extinguished blowtorch turned to extreme apprehension by his captor's next remark. "Following your friend's snooping a week ago, I was obliged to avail myself of some four-legged friends for additional security. As I am sure you are aware, although a Dobermann pinscher can make a lovable pet, lurid wartime stories about how specially trained dogs of this breed were employed in German holiday camps such as Buchenwald still prevail to this day. We are now adjourning to a location nearby where you will confront two of these beasts, whilst I witness from a spectators' gallery whether or not British secret service self-defence skills are effective in dealing with canine predators."

Silently refusing to make plain the terror lurking in his guts, the colonel's intended victim was then frogmarched into an adjacent gymnasium by guards, where two of these potentially deadly hounds wandered aimlessly towards him.

With Wing then shouting 'kill' from a small adjacent balcony, Plotter frantically rushed behind a vaulting horse, to subsequent peals of laughter from his tormentor, who jeered, "I believe that got your attention.

As these beautiful beasts were trained in East Africa, how about my addressing them in Swahili? If you are not familiar with the language, here is your first and last lesson, "*Kuua!*"

With that, both creatures flew into a vicious attack mode and, regardless of his desperate attempts to defend himself, within seven minutes Tony Price's entire body had been mutilated, ripped and clawed. In fact, it was almost a relief when his agony was finally doused by a blood-foamed jaw closing around his throat.

NINE

IN TOTAL IGNORANCE OF THE VILE HAPPENINGS IN Berundi, Jingles had at last gained an opportunity to sort out his domestic life, which included reoccupying the now totally renovated Tedworth Square apartment. He had discovered that his former repugnance at so doing was now salved by the death of Rose's murderer.

Nonetheless, he had somehow forgotten the old adage 'fall for an Irish woman and you take on her family'. This factor became very much manifest on the Tuesday that he moved back in.

Whilst hanging some pictures in the early evening, Richard was summoned to his main door by a persistent ringing of the bell. Having become a trifle incautious following his return to London from the jaws of death, he then inwardly cursed when, on opening the door, he found himself staring down the barrel of a Luger pistol.

The good news was that the weapon was being unsteadily held by a homely looking, rather plump, middle-aged lady, but this was then tempered by the fact that she spoke with a broad Irish accent.

"I have been waiting a long time for this, Mr Blake; are you going to invite me in, or shall I shoot you on your doorstep?"

"It might be a good idea to release your safety catch if you are going to take the latter course, but welcome to my humble abode, anyway."

Although Dick was now feeling more relaxed, he was still mystified by the sudden appearance of this obviously distraught woman, who pointedly remarked as she was shown into the drawing room, "So, smart-arse, we know all about firearms, do we?"

"Only because, like most men of my age, Her Majesty obliged me to waste some of my youth by becoming a militiaman. But do take off your coat, with that ancient shooter in its pocket please, then sit down and tell me what you would like to drink. After we are settled, maybe you could identify yourself and explain why there appears to be some problem between us."

"You are an extremely cheeky young man, but I would like a Guinness if you have one."

"I am afraid not, but I can go one better with a luxury Irish whiskey."

Having received a grunt and a nod as the lady seated herself, whilst Richard poured out two generous measures of Macallan Double Cask, he became somewhat concerned that his uninvited guest might be member of the Riley family. However, having already been promoted from 'smart-arse' to 'young man', and with the drinks

NINE

stimulating a more convivial atmosphere, it transpired that his concerns were unfounded.

"Right, Mr Blake, I am Mary Kean and am here to find out what happened to my darling niece, Rose Gallagher, who was like a daughter to me. She completely went off the map almost two months ago and nobody, least of all your bloody police force, can give me a scrap of information concerning her whereabouts. However, what I do know from past phone calls with her is that you replaced horrible Liam as her boyfriend and that this was her last known address. I am also aware that your recent absence on some form of business trip abroad seems to have coincided with Rose's disappearance. What do you have to say for yourself?"

This was a tricky situation to handle for a number of reasons and called for a tactical response. There was also an unavoidable danger that, unless she had already accepted that Rose had vanished as a result of her demise, Aunty was bound to become deeply shocked and upset when she heard the grisly truth.

"Well, Mrs Kean, I am an insurance man with no interest in politics whatsoever and indifferent to what other people's persuasions may be. Therefore, it did not bother me in the slightest that Rose harboured IRA leanings, which I must say turned out to be infinitely less extreme than the violent convictions of 'horrible Liam'. Also, I did realise that she was becoming increasingly disillusioned with the recent violence in Northern Ireland, as I witnessed her being incredibly distraught when her uncle Semus, to whom you are possibly related, was killed in an Amah bombing incident."

Dick's visitor promptly interjected, "He was my cousin, but the silly bugger should never have insisted on being a Protestant or becoming a constable in the RUC."

"Be that as it may, Mrs Kean, but the tragic event, combined with our already budding relationship, convinced Rose to ditch Liam and move on, at which time I was honoured and overjoyed to accommodate her."

"I am amazed that the pathological madman did not come after you."

"In hindsight, ma'am it is a great pity he did not, as I am well able to take care of myself, but I will continue, if I may, and this is where I fear you may become extremely upset. After I then embarked on my lengthy business trip, the little bastard Riley, who was apparently paranoid over Rose's desertion, waylaid her in the street one night and struck her a fatal blow. He then fled to New York for sanctuary with Noraid, who, on learning of his heinous crime, refused to assist him in any way and, in true Manhattan style, he was shortly then found shot dead in a dockside alley.

Please bear in mind that I have only recently learnt of this tragic scenario via an American friend, one Tony Price, who was a member of Noraid until returning to London a couple of weeks ago. Before then, although I knew that Rose had planned to visit Ireland during my absence, I had been confused and upset by not hearing from her, whilst having no knowledge of her whereabouts. What happened to Rose's body is still a mystery, which I intend to vigorously investigate now that I am back home for a while. I can see that you are deeply distressed by all

NINE

this and please know that I also continue to be mortified. Rose was a truly wonderful girl with whom I was hoping to share a future. I believe that it is time for another drink to express truly heartfelt condolences."

Now patently overwhelmed, Dick's impromptu guest then tearfully embraced him as he was fixing the whiskeys.

"I am so sorry, Richard, and do call me Mary. I now have to accept your confirmation of an event which I have been fervently praying would not be true. If that foul animal, Liam, was not already dead, I swear that I would hunt him down and kill him myself, so help me, God. Although I am an IRA sympathiser, I regret that the cause is now employing too many vicious thugs like Riley. Incidentally, I must now point out that my gun was unloaded. Nonetheless, it did surprise me that it did not seem to intimidate in any way a pampered insurance executive like you. Your national service must have been exacting! I have to leave after this drink as cousin Margery, with whom I have been staying in Putney, is preparing a late supper for me. Thank you for your business card and I have jotted my details down on your notepad here, so let's ensure that we keep in touch. I am certain that you will let me know immediately if you discover the whereabouts of Rose's body."

Within five minutes, the fine Irish lady was wending her way home, with fortunately no knowledge of the true gruesome details surrounding her precious niece's slaying.

Dick realised that he never would have good reason to contact this lady again. Nevertheless, he was highly relieved that, probably due to her grief, she had blindly accepted his version of events which, if they had been true, would automatically have enabled the police to be fully aware of Rose's last resting place!

Having let out a mega sigh of relief after Mary's departure, Richard reflected: *At least that is one conversation which I will not be reporting to Falcon, and thank God I am due to spend a jolly night on the town with Toby tomorrow.*

Regrettably, the 'jolly' aspect of the outing was to be severely diminished!

***

Toby had already set up two negronis in the Ritz's Rivoli bar by the time Richard arrived punctually at 7pm. However, as initial pleasantries were exchanged, it became apparent that his rumbustious companion was not on his normal ebullient form.

"What's up, boss? You are making me feel about as welcome as a turd in a punchbowl."

"At the severe risk of putting a dampener on our evening out, Dick, I must show you a telex which I received this afternoon. Unbelievably, it is from the young Nigerian lady that you mentioned during our chat last Sunday. However, the content contains information of which you should urgently be made aware, even though it might cause you serious distress."

Toby then handed over a copy of the message in question, which read as follows:

NINE

Dear Mr Wellington-Green,

We became close almost three years ago when I worked at Murray's Club, and I have just met a friend of yours, Richard Blake. Although he has been reported missing in Nigeria, I believe he may be back in London. If he is, please tell him that our mutual friend Tony Price has been brutally killed by Col. Wing's guard dogs in Berundi, and I am horrified as I loved him.
Cynthia.

Blake momentarily put his hands over his face and murmured, "I am ninety-nine percent certain that this is true and very current as Tony only flew from Port Harcourt to Berundi the day before yesterday. As these bastards had just done their best to rub me out, McCarthy should never have sent him on such a suicidal mission in the first place. Wing must have decided to just blow the final whistle on him, the filthy swine!"

Toby gripped Richard's shoulder sympathetically. "I am not totally au fait with what you are talking about but am so sorry, old man; I realise that you two were close and certainly know what it is like to lose friends in action. Where the hell is Berundi, anyway?"

"Top left-hand corner of the Congo, and I should report this bloody disaster to McFart-Arse straight away, but I am so fucking furious with him right now that it will have to wait until my nine o'clock phone-in tomorrow morning. Meanwhile, Tony would never have wanted to be guilty of spoiling any kind of a social occasion."

Even more unfortunately, whilst the two of them did their damnedest to make the most of the evening, matters were not proving to be a social occasion for the email's author.

***

When Okafor's staff were heading for home at 5pm as usual, Cynthia was surprised when the office entrance guards ordered her to stay at her desk as the general wished to see her. This would be for an unusual second time in one day, the first being when she had been given the gruesome details of Tony Price's death shortly after her morning arrival.

On eventually being summoned into the staff officer's voluminous suite, the ever-amiable Sammy settled back behind his bulky desk and gave Cynthia a broad welcoming smile. "Do sit down just there, my dear, and I am sorry to keep you so late as I am sure you have Christmas shopping to do. Unfortunately, I became delayed by a frantic call from Mrs Fort Lamy. I knew that the brigadier left early today due to his feeling unwell and assumed that he had probably been swigging too much out of his not-so-secret bottom draw bottle. However, according to his wife, on arriving back home, he was violently ill from both ends and developed agonising stomach pains. Anyway, having then promised the neo-demented woman that I would get Major Matuso, the MO, to drop by promptly, I had some trouble locating him and have only just managed to do so."

The young CSM's slightly puffy eyes conveyed a degree of impatience. "That certainly is not as dramatic as

NINE

your news flash this morning, and I must say that I am not really that interested, sir. To what do I owe the honour of two visits in one day?"

General Okafor's face suddenly turned to stone. "Because I am highly disappointed in you, particularly for your stupidity, which I can partly excuse because you can't help being half Fulani."

Following this insulting jibe, he withdrew what was obviously a copy of Cynthia's earlier London telex message from a draw and spread it on the desk in front of her.

"Has it never remotely occurred to you that your home telex machine is fully monitored? What I totally cannot excuse is that, having become a trusted supporter of my grand design, not only do you fail to fuck any information out of a British spy, but also, having fallen for him, you send this crass open telex to some person in London. Worst of all is that the import of your message is intended for another spy who, if he is still alive, most probably killed one of our key Berundi officer's top assistants.

Thus, so far as I am concerned, you have now proved yourself to be a total liability to the cause and will have to be dealt with accordingly. I am not interested in whether or not you have something to say, and your snivelling and slobbering now probably renders that to be an impossibility. Nonetheless, as you do have one virtue left, which is your beauty, I now intend to cheer you up."

Okafor then withdrew his Webley revolver from its holster. "If you wish to avoid my blowing off both your kneecaps, remove your panties, if any, then pull your skirt right up round your waist and bend over the back of that sofa. As I do not trust your teeth, that position at least offers me a double option in which to stream a warm farewell blessing. Incidentally, your late lover's no doubt ample instrument was gnawed off shortly before his throat was ripped out."

By the time the prolonged violent assault that followed was over, Cynthia's pain and humiliation had inspired intense contempt and loathing. Therefore, when she spotted that her assailant had carelessly left his gun on an adjacent side table, without a second thought, she grabbed it and fired four point-blank shots into him.

Terrifyingly for her, the fusillade had no effect whatsoever upon Okafor, who calmly pulled a Colt automatic pistol from his trouser pocket and shot the desperate lady once through the heart.

By the time the two door guards arrived, Cynthia's corpse was spreadeagled on the floor beside her still smoking gun, with her panties safely stowed in her murderer's pocket.

Knowing that the soldiers would not dare to touch the blank loaded revolver, the remarkably unphased general exclaimed, "Fucking hell, chaps, that was a close one. Crazy bitch took four pot shots at me before I could get to my gun. Good job I forgot to send her on a weaponry training course. What? The MO is due to pop in shortly, so he can sort out this mess. You guys will forget the highly embarrassing event. And I mean forget – on pain of death."

With perfect timing, Major Matuso did show up shortly thereafter to report Fort Lamy's unfortunate demise due to some obscure form of food poisoning.

NINE

He was naturally horrified by the Cynthia situation but agreed with Okafor that, as Nigeria was at last settling down again, from a political perspective, the inexplicable event was better hushed up. To achieve this, he organised a private ambulance which discretely transported the body to an appropriate location for clandestine disposal.

***

"Good day, Falcon, Jingles here. My morning report today will be face to face and as soon as possible, so I shall arrive in your office within half an hour."

The reaction was predictable. "Have you lost your reason? I am the one who decides when you come to see me. Tell me what you have to report and refrain from being insubordinate."

"As one of your famous decisions has just cost Plotter his life, I insist that you do as I suggest."

Preceded by a brief pause, the unexpected response was, "Right, Jingles, 0930 hours here in my office."

From the moment that Richard later seated himself in front of his bristling colonel, he passionately launched into what was initially very much of a one-sided conversation.

"Now, Falcon, read this email, which you will see was received by Toby Wellington-Green yesterday and then kindly remain silent until you have heard what I have to say."

Following the colonel's perusal of the message, Jingles continued his discourse. "As the main person now left who is in a position to know, because I have physically experienced Berundi, I am firmly of the opinion that your Birkbeck investigatory mission via Port Harcourt was grossly ill-conceived. For a start, your MI6 linkman, Hassan Fort Lamy, who happened to have been one of my sergeants in Zaria ten years ago, is a drunken idiot who hasn't a clue what is going on half the time. Conversely, Plotter and I both came to the conclusion that the genial general, Sammy Okafor, is far too smooth to be true, innately crafty and knows precisely what is really going on, most of which appears to be contrary to our interests. The Birkbeck Berundi contact, Unegby, is obviously merely a frontman for what I believe is not a People's Republic of China operation, locally controlled by Colonel Wing, of whom the esteemed president appears to be very much in awe. Taking this into account, with security leaking like a sieve and two attempts on my life, I consider that your dispatching Plotter for a follow-up probe was utterly irresponsible. All it achieved was a plainly foreseeable tragedy and fuck all additional intelligence!

"I will briefly summarise my suggested primary solutions, before you have me arrested. For a start, Gowan and his government should be put under greater pressure to proactively investigate the palpable threat of a disastrous national upheaval and they should start by closely scrutinising General Okafor's activities.

As recruiting, training and fully equipping a small army is a vastly expensive exercise, my Hong Kong theory should be fully explored. Let's face it, thanks to the Suez Canal blockage having created a mega tanker boom, their local ship owners alone are awash with available venture

NINE

capital. If my politically inconvenient belief that Berundi's key financial funding does derive from an organisation within our wealthiest colony, then their contribution could easily be instantly blocked by British colonial legislators. That is all I have to say at this point in time, sir."

Much to Blake's surprise, Falcon did not speak for at least two minutes, and when he did, it was in a subdued tone as he slid a couple of handwritten notes across his blotter. "All points taken with no offence, as they are well reasoned, and I deeply regret Tony Price's cruel passing. However, I must update you with certain further factors which relate to your observations. Meanwhile, this is a translation of my somewhat unhelpful exchange of telexes with your friend on Tuesday, when he was obviously being put under extreme pressure.

So far as the Nigerian hierarchy is concerned, I have been vigilantly pressing them for some positive cooperation, but they are still maintaining a distinct reluctance to in any way spy upon their recently emergent loyal officer corps. Also, as Gowan's realigned government is still in the process of consolidating, his policy concerning anything to do with the ever-unstable and unpredictable Congolese President Mobuto is being soft-pedalled for the time being.

You will, I am sure, be smugly overjoyed to learn that only yesterday the Nigerian diplomatic corps in London advised me that the main reason why they had been pusillanimous over Berundi was their need to check out my Chinese suspicions. The consular officer reckoned that Nigeria's relationship with Red China is infinitely closer than ours and is now convinced that the communists are not involved in any such operation. Also, the impression was given that the People's Republic has no current appetite for getting involved with anything to do with the Congo.

"Therefore, although obviously nothing must be mentioned to the Nigerians for the time being, your colonial assumptions are gaining greater credibility. When I have decided upon how to proceed, as an oriental veteran yourself, it is likely that you will be playing a key role in the next phase of this venture. Otherwise, I am becoming anxious over Brigadier Fort Lamy's current status. I have been unsuccessfully attempting to contact him for some time, which is a cause for concern as he always instantly responds to my messages. Finally, I must ask how on earth Major Wellington-Green became involved with this Cynthia woman."

"She happens to be an exceptionally attractive and sexy Nigerian lady who is now one of Okafor's warrant officers in Port Harcourt. However, prior to her military career, she was working in London as a singer in Murray's Cabaret Club and apparently became close friends with Toby a couple or so years ago. When she was recently recounting her experiences to Plotter and I over a drink the other day, I mentioned Toby's name as I know that he often frequents this particular Soho establishment. Cynthia was very excited over the fact that I was a friend of his, as she obviously had fond memories of their times together and insisted that I passed on her loving wishes when I next see him. It would now appear that she had retained his business card and as ever, romance tends to extend the long arm of coincidence."

NINE

"I believe that 'lust' would be a more appropriate term and am somewhat shocked because, as you know, I recently met Wellington-Green for the first time at the home secretary's country abode with his charming, obviously long-term wife. He also happens to have been the gunnery coordination officer during the D-Day Sword Beach landings, when I was but a lowly Second Lieutenant in the Lincolnshires."

"With respect, sir, the most daunting aspect of this is how CSM Cynthia Izanagi became so swiftly aware of Plotter's heinous murder, particularly bearing in mind that she works closely with our top Nigerian suspect, Okafor."

"Excellent point, Jingles, but your next important task is to accompany me on a visit to the Nigeria High Commission in Northumberland Avenue at 1500 hours tomorrow as I have an appointment there with Consular Officer Henry Igboba. I have already met him briefly, and he appears to be a potential supporter of ours who will be positively influenced by your first-hand input. I will buy you some lunch at a nearby Italian restaurant 'Supremo' at 1330 hours."

At this point, Falcon abruptly terminated the meeting in his normal cursory fashion.

Nonetheless, on departure Richard did wonder if he was at last getting through to this grumpy martinet. However, on further reflection, he decided that this delusion was most probably due to his having now become a marginally more important piece in McCarthy's problematic jigsaw puzzle.

Their reserved but not unfriendly lunch the following day, due mainly to the tasty cuisine, at times verged upon being enjoyable. This was in spite of fresh news just received from an alternative Port Harcourt source, which contained decidedly ominous tidings.

Whilst Fort Lamy had apparently died suddenly of indeterminate food poisoning at his home on Wednesday night, CSM Izanagi had not been seen in the office or at her apartment for over twenty-four hours!

These factors inspired a glib Shakespearian comment from the colonel. "It would appear, Jingles, that things continue to be not well in our State of Denmark!"

Notwithstanding this melancholy sentiment, the subsequent conference at the High Commission turned out to be encouraging, in spite of the fact that it did raise one or two pitfalls to be overcome.

Henry Igboba was a bright, intelligent and seemingly energetic man in his late thirties who, as he belonged to the Yoruba tribe, was not tainted with any Igbo/Biafran stigma.

Having thoughtfully listened to the MI6 presentation, particularly Richard's personal report of the growing volunteer numbers, training facilities and substantial quota of armaments which were present at the Berundi base, he fielded some cogent points.

"First of all, gentlemen, thank you so much for your frank and open input concerning your endeavours on my country's behalf, which are based upon your belief that we are in imminent danger of a Biafran-inspired invasion in conjunction with a domestic uprising. Personally, I find your revelations highly disturbing, especially your observation, Captain Blake, where you are certain that a majority of Berundi's ballistic weaponry matches that which was in use during your fairly recent period of Nigerian service. This factor obviously supports your belief that there is a degree of domestic traitorous collaboration with potential insurgents, especially in General Okafor's service and supplies division. Notwithstanding this, within our newly stabilised government, certainly more nationally sensitive politicians could take a view that your activities are tantamount to a revival of colonial interference. Ironically, another point at issue, which was emphatically supported by the communist Chinese is that, if the project is geared to oriental support, funds for underwriting a task of this magnitude would only be available in Hong Kong. Without wishing to state the obvious, this could mean that the subversion which you are encouraging us to suppress is being backed by entities which are part of your recently diminished empire!"

The raising of this point certainly put a ferocious cat amongst the pigeons and inspired an instant response from Falcon.

"Excuse me butting in, Mr Igboba, but this remote possibility has already occurred to us, and we have an investigatory team working on the matter as we speak. Meanwhile, might I enquire what progress your countrymen have made with probing their Congolese and Cameroon contacts re transportation of the Berundi force, which will, I fear, shortly occur if you further delay taking appropriate positive action?"

Igboba smiled ingratiatingly. "I am relieved to hear your

news concerning Hong Kong, but you have to appreciate that, having just struggled through some traumatic times, Nigeria currently has to tread with extra caution internationally. I personally will do all in my power to assist in averting what I also perceive to be a more than possible disaster waiting to happen. Fortunately, my personal position has recently been strengthened as High Commissioner Maduka Dugary, in order to play down his personal involvement, has seconded the matter for me to deal with.

I regret that I must now bid you farewell, as I am late for another meeting, but please keep closely in touch and supply me with as much ammunition as you can to assist me in achieving what has now become our common cause. Also, do advise me as soon as you can re the Hong Kong situation as that could prove to be a constricting bone of contention."

En route in the taxi, Jingles commented, "Well, Falcon, that went well," which, not unexpectedly, provoked an irascible contrary reaction.

"It was nothing short of a bloody disaster. Nevertheless, it has obliged me to send you off to Hong Kong post-haste and link up with our people there to make an investigation."

"Not over Christmas you won't. I have planned to celebrate in New York all next week."

"Immediately after you get back from the States, then. And do not pester Petal whilst you are out there."

"Actually, Falcon, I shall be staying at her home as an invited guest. I will hop out of the cab right here and grab a tube as I know that you have to don your finery for a meeting with 'the amateurs' at 1730 hours, followed by a fascinating early dinner with lots of hilarious speeches!"

TEN

Having resisted pressure to have his luggage unpacked and stowed for him, Blake dismissed the two zealous Mandarin Hotel floor waiters and sat back in one of the luxurious room's easy chairs in order to relax and review his situation.

It had been a long, tiring journey from London, which he had commenced before fully recovering from 1971 New Year celebrations which immediately preceded his flight back from the States.

Amazingly, Falcon had sanctioned his staying in the best hotel in Hong Kong, which his army superiors had never allowed on his earlier visits to the city. Even the great perfectionist, Toby, who had already urged him to check up on his office and try to produce some useful additional contacts, would have been impressed by his colonial lodging arrangements.

In spite of Petula's devastation over Tony's fatal shooting – true details having been too gruesome to mention – and her mum staying over on Christmas day, Dick's week in New York had been little short of idyllic, and the shadow of commitment was ominously looming!

However, he now had a gruelling task to perform where, for certain technical aspects, he would be obliged to seek the advice and assistance of the local MI6 operative, Robert Campion – code name 'Wander'. This man was so far an unknown quantity, but during Blake's one phone call with him on his arrival, his tone of voice disturbingly came across as condescending.

Fortunately, though, Jingle's first appointment was to have dinner in the hotel roof restaurant with his old friend, Commander Bill Welkin RN, who was shore-based locally on HMS *Tamar*. They had originally become friends whilst sorting out a particularly tricky local drug-related situation three years earlier and had kept in touch ever since.

Apparently, Bill, whose features and body were spreading into early middle age, had now become bored with being 'concrete-based' and was planning to retire and settle down with his family in Cuckfield, Sussex as soon as possible. In a way, this was good news as, when his estranged father was absent, Richard visited his mother in Lindfield village which was only about three miles away.

The dinner, which was preceded by the jaded traveller grabbing a two-hour recuperative nap on his bed cover, turned out to be an interesting and humorously enjoyable event, as usual. Unfortunately, though, Richard's attempt to glean some useful input from his friend concerning his thorny task in hand turned out to be pretty fruitless.

TEN

"It sounds to me, Dick, that you are searching for a commercial needle in a convoluted business haystack. As you know, no bugger pays very much tax in this place, which is great personally but makes life bloody difficult if you are seeking corporate information. Also, any set-up which is dodgy, as this one certainly appears to be, would normally hide behind a foreign entity in somewhere like Switzerland which, as we know, is as tight as a duck's arse when it comes to revealing anything.

I sincerely hope that your bloke Campion has got some influential pals in the government who can be of help as that would appear to be your only hope. I have never actually met the bloke, but I have seen him at cocktail parties, and he has a lofty, hawk-faced air of arrogance about him. Nonetheless, do not forget that if anything involving nastiness has to be done, my Royal Marine thugs are ever on standby."

"Thanks, Bill, but as you have just heard, I had more than my fair share of nastiness, blood and guts during 1970, and I am determined that 1971 will be my year of comparative tranquillity."

"Long may that be so, my friend, but the routes that MI6 follow are not renowned for being the paths of peace!"

Like all successful sailors, the commander turned out to be spot on with his forecast!

Unfortunately, Richard's highly enjoyable Bill Welkin evening was followed at 10am the next day by a decidedly less pleasant encounter with Wander, who opened their discourse with, "For Christ's sake, do not use my ridiculous code name, and I shall be addressing you as Blake, not your fatuous 'Jingles' alias."

"Campion, I don't care if you call me Father Christmas so long as you can use your contacts here to help me nail the information I am seeking."

"Of course. As you will have seen on my door, I represent Lloyd's brokers, Wallis, Lester and Daltry's interests. As such, I have extensive involvement with local corporate and government institutions, particularly in respect of marine matters, as the company insures Hong Kong's two largest shipping fleets in the London market."

This indicated that at least Campion must be reasonably able, but Richard felt disinclined to mention his own marine insurance involvement.

"Right, Campion, I know that you have already received a briefing from McCarthy in London; what are your thoughts?"

"Frankly, Blake, until you stimulate me by supplying more specific information in depth, I am decidedly lukewarm over addressing this somewhat obscure chore."

At this, Richard ran out of patience with the agent's haughty, negative attitude.

"Listen, you are Wander; I am Jingles; and our chief is Falcon, whether you like it or not. I have been part of this particular operation from the beginning, which happens to be of vital importance to UK interests and for which quality individuals unlike you have already sacrificed their lives. I am ordering you to assist me in identifying local companies which have been formed during the past two years, appear to be excessively thriving and, if possible,

TEN

where their profits are invested. Now, think of England and get your arse into gear, as if you do not, I shall report your indifference to Falcon, who I am certain has the power to put paid to your undoubtedly jammy little insurance career, just for starters!"

A chalk white perspiring face, clenched teeth and shaky hands clearly indicated that this message had well and truly got through and an unrecognisably humbler, barely audible voice responded, "I shall get onto the task right away and hopefully have some news for you by 1500 hours, Bla... Jingles."

On returning to the Wallis office at the appointed hour, following a Chinese lunch in a small local restaurant, Richard was surprised, if not a trifle irritated, to observe that Wander had regained much of his egotistical bounce.

"Well, Jingles, I believe that I may have found a solution for your problem, but consummating a deal is likely to involve certain downsides which you may find personally offensive."

This remark left Blake somewhat taken aback. "Well, I have never been accused of being prudish, even in this bizarre part of the world, so kindly elucidate."

"A very nerdy accountant called Han Shan, whose nephew works for me as a clerk, has achieved a spectacular career in government administration and is now their top corporate auditor. Like many unprepossessing people, his job is his life, and he has developed a neo-photographic memory for all the data with which he deals. Thus, if suitably encouraged, he could be the perfect person to help you identify that which you are seeking. Having dealt with him on a couple of previous occasions, it is his idea of being suitably encouraged which you may find unsavoury."

At this point, Richard's mind was racing. "What happened to good old bribery and corruption, for God's sake?"

"I am afraid that he has already got money to burn, but what he will be expecting does not come cheaply if done properly, anyway!"

"Wander, come on, tell me the worst and break my heart."

"Quite simply, Jingles, he is obsessed with the oldest local game in the book, of which I am sure you are aware: Hong Kong Roulette. Shan quirkily insists on partaking in this contest with any person who requires his opinions or assistance."

Blake's marginally hypocritical outrage over this requirement was exacerbated by the smirky manner in which it was proposed.

"I see, Wander, but, along with the devouring of live monkey's brains, this happens to be a practice of which I have always disapproved and in which I have never partaken."

"Well, Jingles, that is entirely up to you, but this guy offers by far the best chance for you to achieve your goal. As you so aptly remarked this morning, 'think of England', but, if you are unwilling to fulfil your duty on this occasion, I will have to cancel the booking that I have arranged for this evening. That is, unless you instantly have a change of heart and decide to go along with Han's

TEN

quirky requirement, when all you have to do this evening is appear to be unperturbable during supper. That should then persuade the little pervert to furnish you with the information you require tomorrow."

Feeling certain that he was being set up by bloody Campion, but realising that beggars cannot be choosers, Jingles duly arrived at the appointed location on the dot of 7pm. Here, Wander introduced him to the gawky, stammering little Mr Shan before downing pre-dinner drinks and adjourning to a private dining room with commodious furniture.

Han and Richard were then sat opposite one another to be tested on who would be the first to make any facial expression, movement or utterance that might have been inspired by pleasures being bestowed upon them beneath the table. Whilst this was performed with dextrousness, Richard was not quite sure who was supposed to win the game, until a scowl from Campion towards the end of the meal prompted him to smile widely and utter a grunting sigh.

Shan was plainly overjoyed and greatly impressed by his adversary's long-term constraint so, having planted a slobbery kiss on the two svelte naked ladies on their emergence from under the table, he insisted upon Blake visiting his office at noon the following day and then departed.

After bidding the now hastily clothed eroticists farewell with a generous emolument, Jingles reseated himself at the table.

"Be sure, Wander, that if any word of this evening's disgraceful, if marginally enjoyable, activities ever gets out, I shall personally cut your balls off. Also, in the event that the twitching little shit fails to come up with something genuinely useful tomorrow, I shall cut them off anyway. Until then, you might be my temporary best friend if you procure a very large Remy Martin for me."

As it had at last occurred to Campion that Blake was probably not an individual with whom to tangle, he readily complied and after yet another round, Richard was on the verge of believing that maybe agent Wander was not such a tosser after all!

The content of Richard's meeting with an intensely business-like Han Shan on the following day dispelled any danger of Campion being obliged to speak in falsetto tones.

Now in his office comfort zone, which was suitably embellished to suit his exalted civil service position, Han had evaluated and defined a myriad of information at his fingertips and come up with a well-reasoned, credible result.

Having tediously talked his guest through the finer details of his corporate analysis, the unquestionably brilliant boffin summarised his findings. "So, Captain Blake, on considering all the points that I have mentioned, there is clearly one company that sticks out like a sore thumb, which is Pin Don Ho Shipping and Finance. With a rapidly growing fleet of now eighteen tankers, they are exceptionally active for a corporation that was formed but two years ago. In addition to this, all their profits appear to be syphoned off into the Godwin Bank of Geneva, which was founded at the same time. Since then, this novice Swiss financial institution has openly acquired substantial shareholdings in the local CY Pew and YK Tang shipping

TEN

lines, who between them own over a hundred tankers and bulk oil carriers. I am afraid I can be of no assistance in respect of the bank's private investments in view of rigid Swiss confidentiality guarantees.

If you have no further questions to pose, as you depart, my secretary will supply you with a file containing all the information that I have amassed on your behalf. From this, you will note that the Pin Don Ho company office is based on Po Toi Island, which, as a matter of interest, is an eight-mile boat ride from Aberdeen. I really hope that my conclusion proves to be correct; if not, do not hesitate to revert when we might have another little supper together."

Having profusely thanked the Han Shan for his efforts, Richard departed with at least one very good reason for not wishing to bother him again!

***

It was now clear that Blake was obliged to become more deeply involved in the marine insurance business again, so having broadly briefed a decidedly more amenable Wander over a beer and some sandwiches, his next port of call was Toby's local office. This was run by one Philip Sprat and fortunately Richard had got the address in his wallet, together with his own business cards, denoting him as a Wellington Insurance Ltd. director.

The compact workplace was in the southern area of the city and, apart from the boss, fielded a local lady secretary and Eustace Tucker, an obvious failed English public schoolboy.

Phil, as he insisted upon being addressed, turned out to be an excessively jolly, rather corpulent, middle-aged man who, having greeted Richard warmly and introduced him to the staff, remarked, "By Jove, sir, I am so glad that you found time to pop in. Toby told me that you might do so, even though your visit to Hong Kong is apparently government-related."

"Actually, I am only here so that you and I can pay an impromptu business call on the newly thriving Pin Don Ho shipping company."

Phil suddenly became less effervescent. "Well, sir, I am sorry to say that I have not got around to seeing those new boys on the block as yet, even though I must admit that their office is nearby on Po Toi Island, which is a couple of miles across the bay. With respect, Captain Blake, what do you mean by impromptu?"

"Well, Phil, I am just grabbing a rare moment of my spare time as Toby especially requested over the phone yesterday that you and I make a cold call to this company. If they are too busy to see us, at least we will have made our mark and should be able to set a date for you to visit them more formally."

Even though the manager appeared to be decidedly uncomfortable with this suggestion, he reluctantly acquiesced. "I fully realise that your time is tight so, as my launch is parked by the jetty just outside and ready to go, we can be over on the island and in Gordon Avenue where the Pin Don Ho office is located in under half an hour."

His UK company director beamed. "Good show, Phil, that's the spirit. By the way, should we manage to secure an immediate meeting with these people, for governmental confidentiality reasons, my name is Tim Tomlin, got it? I will say that I have left my business cards in the hotel."

Blake's off-the-cuff plan for securing an instant survey of what had now become an urgent objective turned out to be too good to be true when the corporate risk manager expressed interest in their operation and interviewed them for half an hour.

Then, to crown it all, they were invited to take tea with the chief executive, a small, bloated man with a cruel mouth in his late thirties called Billy Lo. This was perfect as it enabled Jingles to identify the location of the safe and secure filing cabinets in his elaborate office.

Although Phil had erroneously rechristened Richard Tom Tinkin, unbeknown to the two guests, concealed cameras were in operation during their sojourn as Mr Lo had recently been ordered to report on and record images of all previously unknown visitors.

Following the broker's departure, the prompt exchange of messages with Berundi put him firmly in the picture:

To Albert Unegby. Uninvited visit from Wellington insurance salesmen Philip Sprat and Tom Tinkin (see photo attached). Any comments? Billy Lo.

To Billy Lo. Parties depicted critically dangerous to whole project, especially good-looking younger one who's MI6, real name RICHARD BLAKE. Use all in power to eliminate both as soon as possible and keep me posted. Albert Unegby.

On leaving Po Toi, Phil kindly sailed his launch to the Mandarin's harbour, where Richard invited him in for a drink in the hotel's Captain's Bar.

"God almighty, Phil, thanks for driving me home, but your boat is so bloody noisy that I could hardly hear myself think, let alone speak. I trust you found the meeting useful for the future and I am sorry for springing it on you like that. I must shortly revert to my tight schedule where I will probably be tied up with our Royal Navy boys later this evening and for most of tomorrow."

"Actually, Captain, my launch is making a filthy racket because, like a prat, I reversed her into a rock and snapped off part of the exhaust pipe yesterday. Your old soldier's approach to business production was a real learning curve for me and you can tell Mr Wellington-Green that I shall diligently pursue matters with the company, even though I must admit to you that I did find Mr Lo to be a somewhat sinister character."

Their conversation continued in a more social vein until, following a second round, Blake excused himself as he now urgently needed to speak with Bill Welkin again.

Most frustratingly, on endeavouring to make contact with him via a foyer telephone, he was advised by a *Tamar* petty officer that, as Commander Welkin was on an exercise, he would not be available until around 6pm tomorrow. Thus, with no other immediate plans, Richard decided to be sensible for a change and catch up on his jet lag by grabbing an early night.

Nevertheless, life was rarely completely straightforward and, on returning to the bar for a nightcap following a

TEN

snack in the Mandarin's Moonglow Café, his well-honed instincts telegraphed that he was being watched.

The suspect was a slender, blue-suited, prematurely balding young man with Asian features who was seated at a nearby table, intensely studying the ceiling's main chandelier. Nevertheless, Richard was certain that he had fleetingly observed him secreting what appeared to be a miniature camera in his jacket's side pocket.

On then retiring to his room with his suspicions still lingering, Blake put the Beretta under his pillow when he went to bed, having attached its silencer, and decided to wear it on a regular basis again.

Having then been awakened by the arrival of a late breakfast in his room, he was surprised to receive a message from reception that a Mr Wellington-Green would be telephoning him at 11am. When the call came through, it rapidly became apparent that his chairman was in a highly distressed mood at 4am London time.

"Richard, I do not know what the bloody hell you are up to out there, but whatever it is has nigh on killed a member of my staff."

"My God, Toby, what on earth do you mean?"

"I will tell you precisely what I mean. First of all, just before lunch yesterday I received a somewhat tremulous call from Sprat to report that, on the basis of my say so, you dragged him off to see a ship owner that I have never heard of. Then, during a subsequent surprisingly successful presentation, which included meeting the company's boss, you insisted on assuming a bogus identity. As the dear man was obviously seeking a rarely earnt pat on the back, I made some bland encouraging remarks before putting the matter behind me. That was until two-thirty this morning when I was awakened by a Miss Wong, who works for Sprat in my office out there. She then hysterically wailed that her boss had been all but murdered by a massive power boat deliberately ramming his launch as he was arriving at the office. After considerable histrionics, I gathered that the poor chap had been ambulanced to the MacCauley Emergency Clinic from whom I have been trying to get some sense all night, but where he appears to be still alive. Sadly, his wife has left him, and he has no children.

Nonetheless, you keep well away from him, plus the rest of our staff and contacts, as the assignment in which you are involved appears to have made you a bloody dangerous man with whom to be associated. As you can gather, I am less than pleased with you but, as Sprat's ramming incident was probably staged as a severe warning, for God's sake watch out for yourself, my old friend."

"Toby, all points taken to heart, and I am so sorry to have caused you grief and hopefully only temporary injury to the decent and likable Phil. I will, of course, personally check with the MacCauley Clinic that the poor fellow is still in one piece and likely to remain so."

At which point, the conversation was abruptly terminated, with profuse apologies from a hotel switchboard operator.

Instead of calling Toby back, Blake then spent a frustrating hour establishing with the Emergency Clinic that Mr Sprat would survive without likely permanent injury and ensured that his accommodation was the best

TEN

that they could offer. In all fairness, this could not have been achieved without assistance from Campion, through whom he also organised the stationing of a guard to ensure the patient's security.

Nevertheless, although Richard was now becoming increasingly impressed by Wander's efficiency, he did not deem it necessary to enlighten him concerning his intended offensive plans in collaboration with the Senior Service!

Whilst partaking of a late snack lunch, Blake received a message to the effect that Commander Welkin would meet up with him in the Captain's Bar at 6pm and take him out to dinner.

As his Asian 'photographer' was again stargazing nearby, Richard was rather pleased when Bill turned up in full Royal Naval fig, for which he unnecessarily apologised. "Sorry about showing off, Dick, but to be on time I had to come directly from the *Tamar* base."

"That's fine and great to see you again so soon, but keep your voice down, and we won't talk turkey yet as I have grave suspicions over that bloke in the blue suit over there."

Whilst they later enjoyed an extremely tasty, good old British steak dinner with all the trimmings in the John Bull Brasserie, Welkin was duly brought up to speed with recent events.

"Well, Dick, from this we have to assume that you have probably been rumbled. This means that, as Billy Lo and his gang may now be geared up for trouble, our search raid on the Pin Don Ho office will need to be swiftly done and could be more confrontational than we originally anticipated."

"Precisely, Bill, it would seem that, true to your prediction the other night, a life of tranquillity has eluded me again and I am right back on my old nasty blood and guts course. Anyway, at least I had the chance to suss out our objective yesterday which, apart from a couple of staff loos and some kind of kitchenette, comprises of just two rooms which are about forty by thirty feet each. The entrance leads into the first one which houses six clerical staff, one typist and a receptionist, whilst Mr Lo occupies the other one where all the secure storage cabinets appear to be located, plus a fairly robust-looking safe. I have even created a highly artistic map for you."

As the commander studied Blake's efforts, he queried, "What about the building's security arrangements and other occupants?"

"Good question, Bill, and I was coming onto that. The one-story property appears to house only three other businesses, and there is a small, unmanned reception area with one fairly mature, probably part-time, armed guard. What I did notice, though, was that all the Pin Don Ho windows are barred. We really do now have to get stuck in as soon as possible before someone panics and the documents I so desperately need are destroyed."

"Right, Dick, then I think that we should go in tomorrow night with all guns blazing, plus, if necessary, some chloroform, in case the geriatric guard is on duty. I shall select a suitable up-front team of possibly half a dozen armed thugs who, like me, will be wearing

TEN

mufti. As I am pretty sure that our enemies will now be geared to expect some form of intervention, I intend to secrete a more substantial reserve squad in the vicinity to cover us if we encounter any serious problems. In the meantime, I will advise the Hong Kong constabulary that the navy is pursuing a military exercise in the Po Toi area tomorrow night, which may involve the firing of blank weaponry."

With that, having agreed on some finer points and timings, the two of them rounded off their meal before sharing a nightcap back at the Mandarin, where there was now no sign of the Asian suspect in the bar area.

In general, Blake was not too scrupulous with regularly monitoring his messages but, bearing in mind what had occurred during the past couple of days, after bidding farewell to Bill Welkin, he checked with the hotel reception desk.

Here, the fortunately overzealous liveried clerk, who confirmed to Richard that there was nothing in his pigeonhole, imparted some vitally significant additional information.

"Oh, and by the way, sir, I thought that you should know that an apparent close friend of yours was urgently trying to contact you earlier in the evening and obliged me and my colleagues to telephone your room five times."

With caution alerted, Blake responded, "Thank you, what was his name?"

"Strangely, he did not see fit to leave one, Captain Blake, but he was a thin, olive-skinned, fairly young gentleman."

"Was he wearing a blue suit?"

"Er… I think he might have been. Either blue or green."

As everyone is well aware, no decent hotel would ever divulge the room number of a guest to a third party. However, people intent on securing such information can often do so by asking to be connected to a named occupant's room and observing a desk clerk's dialling pattern.

"You will never know how grateful I am for that information, young man."

The gallant captain was very soon striding purposefully along the corridor to his mini suite, oozing with vengeful incentive. As he did so, he once more mused upon the fact that the only reason fictional heroes, such as 007, survive is that their would-be killers always insist upon indulging in anticipatory gloats.

In reality, the only sure way to terminate the existence of a person whom you consider to be mortally dangerous is to shoot first and then brag about it afterwards!

He was thus intent on making a super-quick hit, the chance of which was enhanced by the Mandarin's adoption of a new magnetic key system where one only had to touch the outside lock plate in order to open the door.

This turned out to be a vital factor as, when Richard suddenly crashed into the room, gun-in-hand, his would-be murderer was sitting in the centre of the drawing room with a heavy calibre automatic pointed straight at him.

Nonetheless, within a fraction of a second, the assassin's balding scull was anointing an elaborate chair cushion with a colourful blend of blood and brains.

Although its silencer had adequately muffled his weapon's discharge, Blake still needed to promptly dispose of the corpse, plus any telltale signs of the killing, and to

TEN

achieve this, he decided that it was time for Wander to be truly put to the test.

"Hullo, old man, it's Jingles here and I am sorry to be phoning you at home so late in the day, but I am having some laundry problems here at the Mandarin which I need you to urgently sort out for me."

Following a brief pause, Campion replied in a barely amiable tone, "I am very sorry, Jingles, I really have not got a clue what you are on about."

"Don't worry, Wander, I simply require you to perform a standard secret service procedure. I have become stuck with the body of an over-optimistic hooligan who unsuccessfully attempted to deprive me of my young life just now.

All you have to do first thing tomorrow morning is disguise yourself as a specialist laundry man, convince whoever is posted at the staff entrance that you are responding to a VIP guest's orders, ascend in the lift and wheel your spacious trolley to room 416. Having then loaded up the somewhat mangled remains of my unwelcome visitor, together with any revealingly stained items, you will depart and dispose of same. Our game is not all bullshit and blow jobs, you know. See you in the morning."

Most fortunately, Campion passed his test with flying colours and was at Richard's door by 9am with a bulky conveyance paradoxically labelled 'LIVE AGAIN Ltd – Specialist Restorers of furs and skins'.

Fortunately, no mention was ever made by the hotel management to Captain Blake concerning the mysterious disappearance of a large chair cushion from his suite.

***

The Pin Don Ho office was situated in a semi-isolated zone, well away from Po Toi Island's domestic area and opposite a small, partly wooded park, where Jingles and Welkin – plus six marine commandos – congregated at 10pm.

"I don't know, Bill, but from what we can see from here, the whole building is in darkness and there does not appear to be anyone covering the reception area. Nonetheless, as we have both learnt, sometimes to our cost, when things appear to be too good to be true, they usually are not. I suggest that one of your chaps checks out the other side of the place and also takes a look at those garages that I have only just noticed to the rear of the plot."

It was just after one of the marines set out to perform this task that events dramatically turned out not to be 'too good to be true' in any way.

Following the solitary sound of a nearby gunshot, Blake's group were suddenly illuminated by a powerful beam of light as a dozen armed men emerged from some trees to their rear.

Simultaneously, a resonant voice addressed them via some form of megaphone in an oriental broken accent.

"Captain Blake, we serve the Pin Don Ho Shipping and Finance company. How could you be stupid enough to believe that you would be permitted to disrupt a vital, multi-million-dollar business that many hard-working people rely upon for their employment and subsistence? The man that you murdered last night has just been avenged by the death of your solitary snooper a moment ago and, assuming that all of you have now been persuaded to discard your weapons, you will follow me."

With that, a stocky man wearing a para-military uniform and carrying a Thompson sub-machine gun stepped out of the adjacent foliage and began walking towards the garage block. Simultaneously, vicious firearm jabbing persuaded Jingles' team to do as they were told, whilst Welkin whispered, "Well, Dick, at least that shot which took out poor old Felton should have alerted my special reserve detachment. If not, I fear that we are about to be plunged into deep shit!"

Fortunately, before reaching their objective, they were rescued from imminent sewage emersion as a staccato voice ordered, "Hit the deck, boys whilst we save your arses."

Within seconds, after three of the aggressors had been wounded and their leader shot dead, twenty or so black-clad troops moved in and, having disarmed the remaining erstwhile captors, secured them in the garages and posted guards.

The initial naval detachment then easily broke into the Pin Don Ho premises and, with their assistance, Welkin and Blake conducted a thorough search of the entire office area.

Most exasperatingly, however, in spite of much latch-forcing and safe-cracking by one of Bill's specialists, they failed to discover any documentation which was remotely incriminating.

That was until, as they were on the point of giving up, Bill glanced inside an unlocked battered cabinet in the corner of the general office and, lo and behold, tucked under a Lloyd's Register tome was a bulky cardboard file labelled 'Berundi/Unegby/Godwin Bank'.

Richard was totally ecstatic when a quick flick through the folder revealed that this was exactly what he desperately needed.

"Bill, I am now totally in your debt, not only because the objective of my mission would never have been achieved without you, but also, if it had not been for your emergency reinforcements, I would most probably now be 'brown bread.'"

"Ever a pleasure, Dick, but I do rely heavily upon what Napoleon often said prior to meeting his Waterloo, 'No one is any use unless they are blessed with luck'. However, on a practical note, as Mr Billy Lo's Pin Don Ho company has technically committed no crime, my activities and those of my men must remain strictly unofficial and deadly secret. Also, I am afraid that Corporal Felton's tragic death will have to be reported as a training exercise accident. Meanwhile, as bumping them all off would not be very sporting, we will leave our imprisoned murdering bastards to their own devices."

"Well, Bill, at least they are going to have lots of fun breaking out of those unusually robust garages. Apart from that, I am certain that Lo will maintain a low profile so far as his office break-in is concerned and steer well clear of involving the police. He will, though, be shitting blue lights over the documentation that I now have, as he knows full well that its exposure is guaranteed to totally scupper the commercial credibility of his company in Hong Kong.

TEN

In any event, I shall be treating you to a slap-up farewell lunch at the Peninsular Court tomorrow as I must now urgently return to London and enlighten the Colonial Office of the damning information contained in this file."

ELEVEN

When Jingles arrived back in London following his five fraught and varied days in Hong Kong, he had little difficulty securing a Falcon meeting, even though he did have to suffer a smattering of his customary cantankerous rigmarole to begin with.

"I trust that there is a damned good reason for you to telephone so late at night, or are you drunk?"

"Even I rarely get plastered by 1700 hours, Falcon."

"Ever the smart-arse. And if you are back in London in under a week, I cannot believe that you have managed to complete your mission to my satisfaction."

"The answers are: I am, and I have."

"I see. Where are you at the moment, then?"

"At my Tedworth Square home, just about to unpack and get some shut-eye."

"In that case, Jingles, I will see you in my office at eight-thirty sharp tomorrow morning. Meanwhile, I will endeavour to arrange an appointment with Igboba later in the day, when, in view of the likely import of your

ELEVEN

revelations, I would expect the high Commissioner to also be in attendance."

As Richard was still feeling the effects of his long flight, it was much to his relief that McCarthy lapsed into a flabbergasted silence as he leafed through the contents of his sequestered file next morning.

The documents contained therein were a date-ordered compilation of mainly telexed messages between Billy Lo, Albert Unegby, cc Berundi National Bank and Gunter Call of the Godwin Bank in Geneva.

Most of them were advices, requests and confirmations of a steadily escalating pattern of payments, all ultimately in favour of Berundi and currently totalling over fifty million pounds.

Even more damning, however, were inserted detailed instructions concerning the type of equipment and/or weaponry which was to be acquired. Furthermore, some of these specifications included deeply incriminating remarks, such as 'to match the ones we received from Nigeria' and 'Nigeria has promised to supply some of those'.

For once, Falcon let his shock and horror show. "My God, Jingles, you were right, that is enough money to start a small war, and as the funding now unquestionably originates from our territory, it must be blocked immediately. I will have my ADC copy all these papers to the colonial secretary and urgently telephone him as well."

"Also, sir, do not forget that the Pin Don Ho-owned Swiss Bank also benefits significantly from their investments in the Hong Kong-based CY Pew and YK

Tang shipping companies who are powerful and will need careful handling."

"I had not forgotten that, Jingles, but, as this has now become a national embarrassment, I shall rely upon you to devise some form of feasible rationalisation when we see the Nigerians in Northumberland Avenue at 1100 hours. This is not just due to your having been very much on the front line in this operation but also because we are now in desperate need of some compelling bullshit, which appears to ooze out of you like rancid honey!"

Much to Richard's relief, when he and his boss checked in at the Nigerian High Commission, only the sympathetic Henry Igboba was present to meet them both in a conference room.

Unfortunately, however, just as the diplomat had finished scanning through his copy of the Berundi file, the door opened abruptly to admit a younger, elegantly attired African gentleman who seemed to be bursting with exuberance.

"Well, Henry, I shall now take over from you, as I am dying to hear what our ex-colonial friends have to report concerning their interference with our independent nation's minor domestic hiccups?"

Whilst shunning a response from Igboba and with his chiselled features wreathed in a patronising smile, the intruder then sat down opposite Falcon and Jingles.

"By the way, gentlemen, I am Maduka Durbar, the Nigerian High Commissioner. Although this is our first personal encounter, I do not believe that the formality of exchanging cards, etcetera, is necessary as we are all aware of each other's identities and I am a stickler for coming to the point via the shortest possible route. Am I to assume, from the sheaf of papers Henry has just finished thumbing through, that you have now identified the Berundi backers and, as our Chinese friends suggested, they emanate from the richest of your few existing colonial outposts?"

Jingles, who was still smarting from the death of his friend and other rigours that he had been obliged to endure, now stepped in regardless with no holds barred.

"Listen, 'Your Highness', or whatever else you might choose to be called, what you suggest happens to be true, and you are bloody lucky that the situation occurred as a result of a British technical oversight. Unlike what many financiers would have done, not least of all your erratic communist pals, we now intend to imminently block this whole unfortunate process once and for all. What you people appear to be choosing to overlook is the blatantly obvious Nigerian collaboration which is happening right under your noses and is graphically illustrated in the recently procured documents Mr Igboba has just been perusing."

"Ah, Captain Blake, Igboba has told me that you have an obsession over the potential disloyalty of General Okafor, but let me tell you categorically that, via his family connections with our revered president, his position is sacrosanct."

At this point, Henry Igboba conveniently opted to cut in.

"Actually, Your Excellency, following the defence minister's general enquiry into the collaboration issue, which was inspired by Colonel McCarthy, some serious charges have now been filed against the general. These were initiated by a statement from one of his office guards who reported that, shortly before Christmas, he had born witness to Okafor gunning down a female warrant officer, theoretically in self-defence. Furthermore, the recently exhumed body of Brigadier Fort Lamy, who was the general's deputy and died of food poisoning on the very same night, was found to contain an arsenic-based substance. As Fort Lamy was an MI6 contact and the slain CSM Cynthia Izanagi was closely involved with the local MI6 operative who had just been killed in Berundi, these happenings obviously put Okafor in an extremely invidious position. In addition, as this general controls military supplies, what I have just read in these—"

"OK, Igboba, that is quite enough of your adverse conjecturing. Colonel McCarthy, in spite of the fact that you have seen fit to leave all the talking to your distinctly undiplomatic sidekick, I naturally intend to immediately examine your file containing the fresh data and take a view accordingly. Also, in spite of the Hong Kong involvement being a major embarrassment to the UK Government, I am obviously obliged to pass everything on to Lagos for their comments and input. In this respect, unless you are contacted directly, we can meet up again when I receive a response."

On leaving the High Commission, a decidedly more relaxed Falcon turned to Jingles and observed, "It is a pity that Henry Igboba's presence was usurped. Nevertheless, I am obliged to admit that our encounter went as well as

ELEVEN

it could have done, in spite of the ghastly Durbar whom, I have to say, you handled more than adequately. So much so that it has earned you another lunch at Supremo. As you have not so far bothered to present me with a full mission report, you can fill me in on any other situations of which I should be aware over our repast."

Having diverted the possibility of further nagging from his irksome superior by promising to deliver a written synopsis to him on the morrow, there was an additional Hong Kong development which Jingles was keen to divulge immediately.

As this concerned further undermining of Pin Don Ho's credibility, he outlined the circumstances following which their hitmen had not only tried to kill him but also attempted to drown Phil Sprat, before following up with the main point.

"Apropos of the latter event, Falcon, I received a most encouraging overnight telex from Wander to the effect that, following considerable prompting from him, the Hong Kong Police had located a fifty-foot power boat, which was fully owned by Pin Don Ho. In addition, this craft has now been positively identified by Eustace Tucker and Belinda Wong as the one which deliberately rammed their boss's launch in front of the office and half killed him."

"Excellent news and more grist to the mill. An attempted murder charge against the targeted company will give our cause an extra boost. Now, finish off your expensive negroni and I shall procure us a bottle of Supremo's superior Frascati."

***

Because, until matters in Nigeria and on the Hong Kong front developed into a more positive, definitive pattern, Richard Blake was effectively on standby, he decided that it was a good time to telephone Wellington-Green and fix up an outing.

"Well, Dick, I'm amazed that you are back from your Hong Kong shenanigans so soon, but I am sure that you achieved what you set out to do and trust that you are keeping that crashingly boring CO of yours off your back. Eva is due to return from Spain in three days' time, so we must touch base promptly before you get sent off on another one of your escapades. I have to chair a bloody board meeting tomorrow afternoon, so let's meet up in Ketners at around seven. My turn, I believe, and in any case, it should be as I am certain that I enjoy a far more generous expense account than you get from old McFart-Arse.

Also, Dick, I must profusely apologise for getting so stroppy over poor old Sprat who, as I am sure you are aware, is making a swift recovery. I do feel somewhat fatherly over him though, as he is one of those blokes who seems to be forever in the shit through no fault of his own, and I am sure that if he swallowed half a crown, he would only cough up sixpence."

"Actually, Toby, I took to him during our brief acquaintance as well and am equally delighted that he is going to be OK. However, the organisation that so viciously injured him, before foolishly sending a now-deceased assassin to settle my hash, is now under police investigation. I will supply you with the full details when we meet up."

Indeed, when the two of them then occupied their table in the prime Soho restaurant the following evening, Richard colourfully recounted the events in which he had recently been involved, which sparked off a host of penetrating questions from his companion.

"Anyway, Toby, having been a misery on our last outing because of poor Tony, I am now being a bore during this one, but at least I have super-embellished our jaunt later on. Before joining you, I phoned Oscar to say that we would probably be popping in tonight and he confidentially advised me that the great comedian Dick Emery has agreed to do a forty-five-minute slot as a surprise artist in the Stork Room's ten o'clock cabaret tonight. I obviously booked the very best table for us so, once the bill is settled here, we should still have plenty of time to get to Swallow Street by cab and enjoy brandies on me whilst watching the show."

"What a brilliant idea, Dick, and I trust that evil Oscar will supply us with some suitable bed-warmers to round off the night, or is that not on now that you have fallen for this Yankee lady?"

"God, Toby, I haven't become that much of a bore."

They both had a good laugh at that and later on were wallowing in more intense humour, as Mr Emery closed off his hilarious act to tumultuous applause.

Then, as their half-full bottle of Dimple Haig was retrieved and Champagne ordered in preparation for new friends, Toby moved closer to Richard with an atypically intense expression on his face.

"I know that we are intent upon enjoying a depraved and irresponsible night on the town, but your revelations over dinner earlier on seriously alarmed me. With the Nigerians now being obliged to face up to their perilous situation and sort it out, a great number of people are likely to become casualties and, as a main player in the thick of it, one of them is highly likely to be you. For Christ's sake, there have been three attempts on your life in as many weeks, purely in the build-up to the main show, which means that you are probably already in more danger than the average soldier is in a war situation. As you appear to have served McCarthy brilliantly already, why not tell him that you have now had enough of being his thriller spy hero and recommence your career with me? In view of your specialist clandestine role, I believe that he will be unable to have you court-martialled for disobeying orders, anyway!"

"I am sure he would probably have me shot, Toby. But you of all people – with your jungle activities against the Japs in Burma, plus the D-Day landings and advance through France under your belt – should understand why I would not dream of pursuing such an option."

"Come on, Dick, you were involved in a fair share of action during your twelve years in the mob, unless you've been telling me fibs."

"Sure, Toby, but only limited bush and jungle conflicts and a few close combat situations, hardly open warfare scenarios like Sword Beach where you were establishing artillery batteries under heavy German bombardment. However, much as I appreciate your concern, I am

ELEVEN

determined to see this job through, if only to avenge the unspeakably horrible death which was inflicted upon my dear friend, Tony Price. Now let us regain our sense of priorities and entertain some ladies."

Unfortunately, Dick's Amanda then had to be replaced by an alternative temporary friend as, whilst dancing closely to her, she appeared to be sporting a rock-hard bulge in her nether regions.

However, this ill-judged ploy did produce a substantial monetary saving when Toby and Dick forced Oscar to absorb the Champagne bill as a punishment for his audacious prank.

This deprivation caused the roguish pimp's pointed beard to twitch with outrage as he uttered a bitter rebuke. "You would be amazed at how many City blokes do not complain about my ladyboys, and I am sure that I will eventually catch you two out next time you get properly plastered."

"Don't bank on it," was the simultaneous reply from Richard and Toby!

***

It was but two days later when Falcon received a priority message directly from the Nigerian Government in Lagos. This was marked to be decoded at the Nigeria High Commission, where a familiarisation of the coding structure for future messages was also imparted.

The sender was Special Affairs Minister Victor Adesola, of whom Igboba had never heard, and read as follows:

> *colonel mccarthy investigative info much appreciated being acted upon*
> *some success identity of subversives okafor in interrogation*
> *urgently need blake report to me in lagos as full picture at his fingertips*
> *hopefully he can work with Nigerian government now primary mission*
> *newly appointed special affairs minister victor adesola*

"So, Jingles, it would appear from this communication that our Nigerian friends have woken up at last and are keen for you to support and advise them in their remedial venture."

Blake passed the transcript back to the colonel across his desk. "Falcon, I really do not see how I would be able to assist them further in sorting out their traitors."

"I raised the same point with Igboba at the High Commission yesterday, who reasonably emphasised that you have a unique value in being the only person who has first-hand knowledge of the Berundi base's layout. He also advised me that Adesola's military right-hand man Colonel Colin McMillan is insisting upon your presence."

"My God, Falcon, if this is the officer I think it might be, I shared a thatched hut with him in Kaduna when he was a National Service officer in 1959, and the man is a raving lunatic. You may remember the considerable press publicity when, following his demobilisation and in company with another nutcase, Major Fuller, he rode from Kano via the Sahara to Dakar. Then, having taken a boat to Gibraltar, continued, also on horseback, all the way to London."

"I have no idea what you are talking about, Jingles, but I do find it extraordinary that another officer with whom you previously served in Nigeria has turned up out of the blue. McMillan appears to have more generous memories of you and, since signing on in the independent Nigerian Army, he has obviously become a main man of events—"

"Don't get me wrong, sir," Blake interrupted, "Lieutenant McMillan was a fine soldier, but we just did a number of crazy things together. I remember on—"

There was an instant counter-interruption. "Firstly, do stop butting in; secondly, I am not remotely interested in your trifling subaltern stories; and thirdly, you will be flying to Lagos next Monday with the rank of major.

TWELVE

As the motorcycle-escorted staff car, which had met him on the runway following his BOAC London flight, swept through the traffic into Lagos, it was clear to Major Blake that the city had been substantially embellished since his last visit ten years earlier.

Although some of them were probably still part of ghettoes, in general the former dilapidated buildings appeared to have been replaced by far more sophisticated edifices, a number of which could have structurally competed with the Manhattan skyline.

It was at one of these skyscrapers that Richard was eventually dropped off, where he was greeted by a smartly besuited young African with an enamelled Nigerian flag in his buttonhole.

"Major Blake, I am Alex Aribo, PA to Special Affairs Minister Mr Victor Adesola – welcome to Lagos. We have arranged accommodation for you at our best hotel, The Blu Orchid, where your luggage will be taken immediately

TWELVE

and deposited in your suite. Please be so kind as to accompany me, sir."

Having acknowledged Aribo and followed him through the building's revolving doors, the new major was feeling satisfied with the way things appeared to be going and keenly looking forward to seeing his old friend Colin again. However, this was apparently not now going to happen before he had been escorted into the hallowed presence of the new special affairs minister.

Mercifully, unlike the general international run of senior politicians, Victor Adesola turned out to be a fairly unassuming, squat, mousy man who occupied a surprisingly basic office on the tower's top floor.

Following a brief introduction from the eager Aribo, Richard was soon comfortably seated by the pleasantly friendly minister's desk with a cup of coffee.

"I am delighted that you were able to make it over here, Major Blake, as, thanks in no small part to the input of your countrymen, this embarrassing treachery has bubbled to the surface, and you appear to be the officer that has been most closely involved so far. Also, at considerable personal risk to yourself and following the tragic demise of your colleague, you are now the only person on our side who has first-hand knowledge of Berundi's topography and military capability. These qualifications are greatly embellished by the fact that Colonel McMillan, with whom you have already served and who is the officer I rely upon for martial advice and sensitive security activities, has total confidence in your soldierly skills.

President Gowan has now made me responsible for sorting out this seditious mess where, largely thanks to the efforts of your ex-comrade, we have already identified and successfully interrogated numerous defectors. Colin is joining us for a sandwich lunch shortly and will be taking you to visit one of these traitors this afternoon. By the way, do call me Victor, and I will call you Richard, if that is OK."

Sadly, when Colonel McMillan did arrive to share the snack lunch, it was immediately apparent that his former happy-go-lucky attitude to life was no more.

Not only had the beaky face that topped his gangling, bony body become far more tight-lipped, but also his whole manner exuded an air of haughtiness.

In addition to this, he then reacted with minimal humour when Richard endeavoured to liven up the mundane sandwich munching conversation by alluding to quirky moments that they had shared during their earlier days together.

In fact, Colin only brightened up slightly when he was asked who the mystery bad boy was that they were both due to visit after lunch.

"Ah, Dick, that is my little 'getting back together again' surprise. Wait and see; you will not be disappointed."

Prior to their departure, Blake did take time to brief both of them on the progress in blocking the Pin Don Ho/Godwin Bank's Berundi funding where the Colonial Office had at last got their act together and were making good progress in effecting a clamp down.

Something of which the Nigerians did not seem to have been made aware was that, thanks to the Hong Kong

TWELVE

Police, Pin Don Ho were temporarily stymied anyway due to them having been charged with the attempted murder of Philip Sprat.

"A few British red faces over that whole situation, I bet!" McMillan rather unkindly interjected, to which Blake swiftly retorted, "I believe that there are good reasons for red faces on three zones of the globe for this debacle."

Victor Adesola refrained from making any further comments as he escorted his top hitmen to the lifts and bid them adieu.

As they were descending, Colin remarked, "Time for your treat, Dick, for which we are using a small civilian car, which is parked just outside."

During the short journey that followed, they were driven into an infinitely less salubrious area of the town, eventually coming to a halt outside a grey-brick, sparsely windowed two-story building.

As the two of them alighted, Colin told the driver to wait in a small car park across the road, where they would find him later on.

"Sorry if this all seems a bit cloak-and-dagger, Major, but until we have identified all these subversive bastards, one can't be too careful. As such, this is my hopefully anonymous special prison where we hold suspects for questioning and frequently manage to stimulate confessions and useful enlightenments."

Blake was beginning to become uncomfortable with the direction in which events were moving. A feeling that became distinctly intensified when, having passed through two heavily guarded gates and lead down a flight of stone steps, he became aware of not only sounds of human suffering but also the bitter odour of excrement.

As he was on the verge of raising an objection, however, his escort cut in with, "Relax, my friend, I am just about to reintroduce you to your old pal from Port Harcourt."

With that, he signalled a sentinel to unlock one of numerous barred doors.

"And here is our prime guest who, apart from being a sworn enemy of the state, instigated the gruesome death of our old friend Tony Price, before poisoning your MI6 agent and gunning down CSM Cynthia Izanagi. A real charmer indeed, who, as you will observe, was initially somewhat uncooperative in answering a few simple questions."

In spite of his hideous crimes, Blake found it impossible to relish the state of the naked remnant of a man that was chained to a blood and dung-stained pallet before him.

With his teeth and one eye missing, ribs and a femur obviously fractured, plus numerous missing toe and fingernails and his testicles in tatters, it was amazing that ex-General Okafor was still alive.

Nevertheless, he did manage to maniacally scream, "Hounds… hounds… bit off his cock and face before his throat. Should have got you in Jos. Hah!"

To Richard's horror and shock, McMillan seemed to find this highly amusing as he slashed Okafor round the head with his swagger stick a few times.

"Well, Major, you will be delighted to hear that this heap of shit did betray many of his co-conspirators in the

TWELVE

end, so to give him a break we have got him a date with the hangman tomorrow. Do feel free, though, to rip off a fingernail or two for that last remark. We have some tweezers available on the bench here!"

By now, Blake's dumbfoundedness was lapsing into outrage.

"Thanks for the offer, Colin, but all I want to do now is get out of this hellhole. Then I insist that we go straight to the Blu Orchid hotel, have a great deal to drink and indulge in a highly overdue heart to heart, as you are blatantly in need of some auld lang syne."

"I have a horrible feeling that this visit has failed to amuse you. Have you gone soft or something?"

"The answers to your two questions, Colonel, are yes and no, in that order."

During the short ride to his hotel, Major Blake deemed it inappropriate to express his views on their recent encounter in front of the driver, but he did ask McMillan one question.

"How come that Okafor is now assumed to have cold-bloodedly murdered Cynthia? I was led to believe that she had taken several pot shots at him prior to him shooting her in self-defence and that this had all been witnessed."

"No, Richard, the office door guard had indeed confirmed that she had fired a revolver, which was still smoking by her body. Nevertheless, on later searching Okafor's office when we commenced our investigations, no discharged bullets were found imbedded in either the walls or the furnishings. Thus, it is assumed that the general somehow tricked her into using a gun loaded with blanks."

That may be, Colin, but what the hell can his motive have been?"

"Well, I was coming round to that later because the answer to that question very much involves your good self. When Okafor's office was searched, a pretty damning copy of an email sent from the victim's home and dated on the day of her death was discovered in his top drawer."

"Oh my God, don't bother to continue, this was a message directed to me via a chap called Wellington-Green which concerned Tony's murder and, in the circumstances of which we have now become aware, would have been perceived as treachery. The bastard must have been tracking Cynthia's domestic messaging systems. Another tragedy, as she was a beautiful girl with a marvellous personality."

"So, Dick, it sounds as if you fancied her. You haven't changed much."

"Sadly, Colin, you apparently have, but we can discuss that shortly over a drink or ten after we arrive at the hotel."

As it was still only mid-afternoon, the Blue Orchid's Violet Bar was virtually bereft of patrons as the two officers settled at a corner table with their extra-large scotches on the rocks, and Blake opened the batting.

"You know, Colin, I was really looking forward to seeing you again after all this time, but I have to say, particularly after that revolting display just now, that my eagerness has rapidly waned."

As the colonel made to reply, Blake raised his hand. "No, let me finish. During the eleven or so years since

TWELVE

we last met, I have been involved with the death and discomfort of numerous human beings. Nonetheless, regret has always been my main sentiment for having to do so, never personal gratification. Combatting any form of sedition is ever the trickier side of soldiering, where innocent parties, sometimes including family members, are often at risk from surreptitious assaults. God knows, the Black Watch hardly acted as nursemaids to the Mau Mau when they were sorting out that vicious lot.

Today, however, whether or not your medieval methods might be justified in the interests of preserving the safety of innocent people, you appeared to be sadistically wallowing in witnessing the result of their utilisation. This, I am extremely sad to say, means that the generous, humorous Colin McMillan I used to know may have become a vicious and embittered person, but I fervently hope that I am mistaken in that assumption."

Dick's old companion sat in silent contemplation for a full three minutes before volunteering, "Embittered is most probably the most appropriate description of my present frame of mind. You cannot imagine the horrors that I had to witness during the Biafran conflicts when many of our old Nigerian friends and associates died in horrific ways. Damn it, the Igbos even managed to chop your friend Sokoto up into little bits, which they then disposed of in garbage cans. Let's face it, Africa is a savage continent, and I am sure you will remember what we used to believe was Tony Price's fate in the Congo."

"Well, Colin, I would say that the method recently employed by an oriental sadist for his actual demise was equally as shocking. Nevertheless, even though Tony and I were close friends, I am sure that that he would never have wanted the savagery of his death to turn me into a blindly vengeful psychopath. You may be the boss, Colonel, but as we now have one hell of a job to perform, maintaining a sense of humour will be a vital necessity, and my immediate priority is to revive yours. As my service time has been far more geographically varied than your own, I can assure you that the horrors you have experienced in Africa are no worse than those which occur elsewhere in the world, which very much includes Uncle Sam.

"Anyway, I have now had my say, so let's stop being boring and enjoy our first piss-up for far too long. How about when you and I removed a Japanese anti-tank gun from its war memorial plinth and ranged it up behind a hedge during the monthly Mess Night gathering in order to fire grapefruit that we had jammed down the barrel at the assembled throng. As the breechblock was missing, we used our feet to seal the detonation, which you had overloaded by using three thunderflashes instead of two. The result was then spectacular: not only were all our superior officers' white mess kits covered in shit and fruit fragments, but also the excessive back blast disintegrated one of your mosquito boots and ripped off a leg of my trousers. To cap it all, in the belief that we were under attack, the military band – plus many of the mess waiters – fled and were not seen again all night. I don't remember how many additional orderly officer duties pompous old Colonel Mountain later awarded us, but I still reckon that they were all well worth it. Now stop laughing before you hurt yourself, and l will get us another drink."

TWELVE

***

Following the upbeat close to the turbulent first day of Blake and McMillan's reunion, their former fond friendship was steadily restored.

This revitalised bonding was especially important as, in order to perform their highly exacting mission with zest and ingenuity, it was vital for them to maintain a high degree of synergy.

Their first priority was to assess the availability of skilled soldiery and evaluate weaponry and equipment where, in spite of recent intermittent civil conflicts, the Nigerian Army's arsenal was a trifle antiquated.

In addition to this, although Nigerian Air Force squadrons had recently been nominally expanded by a few Russian aeroplanes as part of a communist effort to perpetuate Biafran upheavals, aside from some British jet fighters, other aircraft were scarce and varied.

Having vigorously pursued these appraisals, exactly one week after Major Blake's arrival in Lagos, he and Colonel McMillan were ready to present a plan to the special affairs minister at 2pm in his office.

Having cursorily inspected Blake's diagram of the Berundi objective which had been mounted on a display board, Minister Adesola greeted his team leaders.

"Well, you two have certainly been incredibly active over the past seven days, during which time, Colin, I observed that you also made a couple of helicopter trips up to Zaria."

"I did indeed, Victor, and there were two main reasons for this. As Richard correctly pointed out on his arrival, we really do not have any more time to spare for seeking out existing subversives. Although I am maintaining my team of informers, just in case there are still some traitors lurking in the bush, Zaria will be a far more discrete location for us to develop our strategies. Also, in addition to being the most abundantly equipped training base, it is located in the North which will eventually be the most suitable point of departure. You have already observed that Dick has sketched out a chart of our objective and, in view of his personal knowledge of the zone, I have requested him to outline our envisaged attack strategy."

Blake duly stepped forward, pointer in hand. "I shall start off by saying that I have no intention of adhering to any form of official military rhetoric as the mission that we are tasked to achieve is far from straightforward and will need perfect planning and fine timing in order for it to be accomplished. As you will see from the size of the accommodation blocks in my reasonably accurate depiction here, enemy numbers are likely to be copious, possibly as many as two thousand or more. Nevertheless, even though a small proportion of the opposing force is comprised of skilled soldiers, many of them will be recruits in training which will obviously be very much to our advantage. Subject to our hitting them hard, fast and by surprise, the novice majority are likely to be falling over one another in panic and confusion, which is bound to significantly hamper the more skilled minority. Because distance dictates that we will be fielding a numerically inferior force, a sudden and subtle mode of attack is an especially essential ingredient of our game plan.

TWELVE

Unfortunately, in order to achieve optimum impact, we urgently need some equipment refurbishment and, of equal importance, an immediate specialised retraining of the relatively mediocre troops currently available. When all this is achieved, what we intend to undertake is a two-pronged night attack.

Force A, the first contingent, will be a detachment of three hundred crack motorised infantrymen under Colonel McMillan, which will advance from Quala airport into Berundi territory. Having abandoned their transports a mile and a half from the enemy encampment, the force will then cautiously proceed to spread out along the western section of its intermittent, low, encircling wall.

Once they are in place, Force B, comprised of two waves of fifty paratroops apiece and under my overall command, will then fly in from Quala and perform a surprise low-level drop focused upon the base's spacious central parade ground area. Their immediate task will be to heavily bombard all the accommodation blocks, especially this one which is occupied by the oriental instructors, via the use of anti-tank rockets and projected incendiary grenades. Simultaneously, Force A will blast their way through any machine-gun posts and defence screens which may be in place, before crossing the nominal perimeter wall and reinforcing Force B in mopping up any remaining enemy resistance."

Victor decided that it was now time for him to interject.

"Well, Richard, that all sounds very straightforward, if a trifle optimistic, but firstly, how about your transport plans? And secondly, what specifically are the personnel quality boosts which you insist are necessary?"

Colin then half raised his hand. "I believe that I should probably come in here as it was my job to inspect the Nigerian Air Force's eclectic fleet of aircraft. I was relieved to observe that not all the fighter planes are Russian as we still retain some good old Gloucester Meteors. However, in relation to our immediate needs, thank God that they have a couple of Handley Page Hastings planes which will adequately cater for the vital parachute drops. More amazingly, however, and with no idea of where the hell they came from, I discovered at the back of a hanger two undusted and unloved American Douglas C-33 Cargomasters. As they each boast a fifty-ton capacity and one of them is fitted with seats, they will comfortably cope with Force A's host, plus their motorised transports. Also, because the airfield at Quala is in the middle of flat laterite semi-desert, the long landing space that these monsters need will pose no problems, even though the run-in may be a trifle bumpy! I have to emphasise, however, that all four aircraft are in urgent need of reconditioning before they can safely fly anywhere."

Richard decided that it was his turn again. "Thanks for covering my refurbishment issue, Colin, and I will now respond to Victor's query over my second requirement in respect of troop quality. Although Colin's soldiery contains a fine bunch of well-trained and hardened fighting men, we both very much doubt the capability of our paratroop force to perform the precision minimum level task upon which we are obliged to rely. Therefore, whilst the Cargomasters and Hastings are being overhauled and Colin is fine-tuning his task force, I am flying to London. My ambitious aim there will be to procure the temporary secondment of a

TWELVE

Parachute Regiment echelon who will hone our heroes and jump with them in order to fulfil the crucial need for accurate landings in the constricted Berundi barracks area.

In the meantime, Minister, you and your diplomats will be engaged in secretly obtaining permission from the Central African Republic for Nigeria to utilise their Quala airport for military purposes."

Adesola smiled benignly. "Our relationship with the country is fairly good at present, but I am certain that sweetening the devilish President Jean-Bedel Bokasso's Swiss tooth will do the trick, anyway. Aside from that, the CAR is currently at extreme loggerheads with the Congo, of which they regard Berundi as being a part; thus, our offensive plans will be much applauded."

This observance was followed up by a question in a less jocular tone. "Why don't we forget all these elaborate tactics and just bomb the hell out of the bastards?"

Colin was obviously eager to respond to this penetrating question. "Well, I believe dropping bombs so near to the Congolese border would seriously overstretch President Mobuto's sense of humour, for which neither the Nigerian Government, nor the UN would thank any of us. Additionally, on the humane UK's behalf, my friend here is more concerned over the well-being of three hundred civilian male and female slaves who are undergoing training in an adjacent complex."

At this, Victor sarcastically observed. "Well, it did not seem to bother you too much with the Germans during World War II."

Richard gave the minister a benevolent smile. "That was very different – they were racists!"

THIRTEEN

"I AM NOT ENTERTAINING YOUR PRESENCE BECAUSE OF your top priority request for my assistance. Particularly as you just decided to waft over here when you are supposed to be assisting Minister Adesola to put this Berundi business to bed before the rebels secure fresh backers. Some of my sources have already suggested that, in exchange for lucrative oil concessions, President Mobuto may already be a keen contender.

Officially, I am no longer directly involved with this Nigerian mission and my sole reason for entertaining your insubordinate presence is to discover how you and Colonel McMillan propose to tackle this festering crisis."

This was Falcon's opening blast when Jingles arrived for a 9am meeting in his MI6 office, barely two days after the strategy presentation to Victor Adesola in Lagos.

True to form, the colonel's favourite butt ignored his bullying tactics.

"Right, Falcon, in that case, I shall defer my priority request as it will become apparent when I put you fully

THIRTEEN

in the picture concerning the plan of attack that Colin and I have devised. If we might adjourn to your small conference room next door, I will affix a map of the Berundi targeted area to the board and give you a detailed briefing. Questions at the end, if you please, sir!"

Having then spent an uninterrupted twenty minutes enlightening the martinet, Blake rounded off with, "So, you will now observe, Falcon, that no time is being wasted via my 'wafting over here' because the restoration work on the aircraft, plus test flights, will take at least ten days. As I am sure you will have observed, the main key to the success of this operation relies upon surprise precision landings by paratroops. In this regard I have to admit that, although the rank and file Nigerian infantrymen are competent, their qualities do not include sophisticated parachuting skills. Thus, my top-priority request is that you assist me in recruiting a fifty-man team from our Parachute Regiment to train, jump with and help me lead the Nigerian airborne soldiers."

If ever anyone experienced a dumbfoundedness, Blake certainly did at this point as McCarthy silently stared at him in apparent shock for at least sixty seconds.

"Jingles, all I can say is that your prognosis does not even deserve the flattery of any sensible questions. Your proposed foolhardy strategies utterly defy logic, and I am inclined to believe that you and your comrade McMillan have gone, what old colonials used to call, 'bush'. I consider that, even with the support of an expert para echelon, if your vital reliance upon the element of surprise fails to work, there is every chance that you will end up grossly outnumbered and outgunned. Thus,

I have no intention of becoming involved with encouraging skilled soldiers to risk their lives by participating in your madcap, suicidal enterprise."

Blake was more than somewhat offended by his superior's damningly negative attitude.

"I would say that the numerous spectacular achievements in Britain's martial past, where quality has outweighed quantity, tend to contradict your pessimistic assumptions, Falcon. Take Agincourt for example!"

Nerves had now been well and truly trampled upon, as the colonel's face turned puce. "How dare you argue with me and presume to give history lessons to someone who was slaughtering Huns when you were still in nappies," he bellowed, before spluttering and continuing his response in a more moderate tone.

"Nevertheless, as I mentioned earlier, I am no longer in a position to intervene as, apart from your secondment, this is now a fully Nigerian venture. In order to prove me wrong before getting yourself killed, you have my blessing to contact some of your more senior old army associates for their evaluation and assistance. I shall be fascinated to hear what their opinions might be concerning your crazy scheme."

"Fair enough, Falcon, that is precisely what I intend to do."

***

It did not take Richard long to locate his former commanding officer, whose availability initially appeared to be irritatingly limited.

THIRTEEN

According to Captain Melrose, his Royal Fusiliers adjutant, the colonel was temporarily based in Salisbury where he was involved with army manoeuvres. However, having further checked this out, the captain called back to say that Barnham was now on leave in London for a week, where he was staying at the Howard Hotel.

When Richard eventually got through to him on the phone at around noon, his earpiece exploded with bonhomie. "Well, about bloody time too. It really is great to hear from you again. I was afraid that you would be pissed off with me for getting you into the OSR, where a little bird tells me that you became so valuable to Her Majesty that your Lloyd's career had to be abandoned in view of the fact that the real 'cloak-and-dagger brigade' cannot function without you. Believe it or not, the little bird and I are dining here at my hotel tonight and, if you are anywhere near town, I insist that you join us."

"I am just off the King's Road as we speak, Bill and, assuming that your wee feathered friend is our mutual pal, Toby, I shall be delighted and honoured to join you. However, as I am on but a brief visit from Africa, where I have been lumbered with orchestrating a challenging little campaign, I desperately need to be tedious at some stage of the evening and pick both your brains.

I believe that the Howard Hotel is the one on the Embankment which overlooks Scott of the Antarctic's steam-sailor *Discovery* and, as I hear that it is an infamous afternoon resting haven for bosses and secretaries, our little bird should feel very much at home."

The colonel burst into raucous laughter. "I am

delighted to observe that you are as outrageous and disrespectful as ever and certain that the details of your craving for military enlightenment will be fascinating. See you in the bar on the ground floor at seven."

Bill and Toby were already getting stuck into their first drink when Richard arrived and a highly convivial evening was soon under way with much hilarity and leg-pulling by his older compatriots, particularly over the fact that he was carrying an attaché case.

When the coffees and Remy Martins had been ordered, Toby remarked, "Well, as I am sure that we are going on somewhere, before we get half-smashed I suggest that Dick unveils what is contained in his school satchel and lets us know what is on his mind."

Richard then discretely slid his slim portmanteau onto the table. "Well, gentlemen, normally I would not be so gauche but, as I am tight on time, I must take advantage of being in the company of two experienced fighting men. I therefore propose to set before you my plans for an assault upon a substantial compound which I shall be jointly heading up for the Nigerian Army very soon. Apart from seeking your comments re general credibility, I urgently need you, Bill, to assist me in temporarily securing and seconding a fifty-man Parachute Regiment detachment to take part in this operation."

During the briefing that then followed, two faces grew sterner, and three brandies remained untouched until they were hurriedly gulped down upon its completion.

Following a short break, during which refills were ordered, Toby volunteered, "So, Bill, as, thanks to you,

THIRTEEN

Richard's MI6 boss is that vindictive shit McCarthy, I believe our first question should be, what does he think of all this?"

Blake grimaced ruefully. "Strictly speaking, as this is now a Nigerian Army operation, it is outside his authority but, to give you a straight answer, he considers my intended strategies to be an over-optimistic load of crap. He also refuses to assist me in securing the vital specialist para force."

Toby's jaw jutted. "If that is McCarthy's view, I would back you on principle; nonetheless, I do believe that you are attempting a bit of a long shot, where you appear to be a tad tight on numbers. What do you think, Bill?"

Barnham manfully endeavoured to look more enthusiastic than he felt. "Well, Dick, you have certainly catered for excessively tight personnel margins, but, as is often the case, success will very much depend on the quality of your rank and file that you are fielding."

Blake perked up somewhat. "In that respect, I can honestly say that, due in no small part to the recent Biafran conflicts, most of McMillan's soldiers are well trained, have had limited battle experience and, apart from airborne proficiency, are generally skilled. So far as numbers are concerned, point well taken, as we could easily be confronted by a force which exceeds my estimated two thousand men. This obviously means that, if our vital surprise element fails, my boys could be exposed to an invidious predicament. I do believe, however, that in spite of capacity needed for shipping the personnel carriers, at least another one hundred soldiers could be squeezed into the Douglas Cargomasters so, in view of your comments, that is something I now intend to do."

Toby interjected, "Christ almighty, your Yankee transport planes must be real monsters and certainly were not around during my years of service. Nevertheless, as this Shen Wing fellow appears to be capable of fielding a basic professional force and many of his recruits will not be at the raw stage of their training, do squeeze in as many extra men if you can as I am certain you are going to need them. Then, if your Nigerians are as competent as you say, with surprise on your side and a fair wind behind you, I reckon that you might have a fifty per cent chance of success. As D-Day was only given a forty per cent chance, so long as Bill can bag you some paras, go for it."

It was now Barnham's turn to cut in, "Hey, wait a minute, Dick, what is all this bollocks about your leading the Force B landings? I can see why it makes sense as you will be the only soldier who has previously seen 'toy town', but when we were serving together, you assiduously avoided any operations which involved your having to use a parachute."

"Touché, Colonel, but for this assault, 'needs must' rules my roost, and I intend to urgently fit in some intensive training in this respect as soon as possible."

Bill beamed as he banged the table. "Bingo, Major, this is exactly how we are going to open the door to securing your specialist echelon. I have a particularly close paratroop pal, Major Jack Elliot, who is based in Aldershot, and I shall request him, as a personal favour, to give you a crash course in precision parachute jumping. As he is fundamentally a reckless, drunken philanderer, I am certain that you two will get on like a house on fire.

THIRTEEN

So, if you play your cards right, this should lay the ground for you to pop the question concerning your temporary secondment requirement and, when he inevitably checks out your request with me, I will give it my cautious support."

"Thanks a million, Bill, that is a bloody brilliant idea which I will go for one hundred per cent. Does your support have to be 'cautious', though?"

"Come on, Richard, in all conscience of course it has to be, as your scheme verges on madness. However, on getting to know Jack, you will realise that the precariousness of your strategies will titillate his desire to be involved, due to his manic Churchillian craving for danger."

Wellington-Green was by now becoming a trifle restless. "OK, Bill, you seem to have very generously provided Dick with a solution for his ambitious predicament whilst I have hopefully persuaded him to reinforce his foolhardy mini army. Miranda's Club reputedly has a new highly imaginative late-night cabaret, so let us have one for the road before pursuing some tactical planning in a more sensual environment!"

***

Major Blake's intensely concentrated seven-day course at the Parachute Regiment's Aldershot base was an extraordinarily contrasting experience between performing actions that he dreaded whilst masking his fear and the enjoyment of being tutored by a truly adroit expert.

In line with Bill Barnham's description, Jack Elliot turned out to be a dapper, handsome ball of boundless energy with a great flare for the enjoying of all aspects of life, thus he and Richard Blake did get on famously.

His opening remark on their first meeting had been, "So, Dick, you come as somewhat of a tall order. If, however, our mutual friend Bill wants you to be put through a normally thirty-day course in a week, I shall undertake a task that I have not performed for a few years and train you personally. This will include kicking your arse out of the plane on your first jump if you show any reluctance. If that is clear and acceptable, let's get cracking!"

"All clear and acceptable, Jack, so long as none of my limbs get cracking as well and spoil my forthcoming African confrontation," was Dick's response as he sewed the initial seeds of his ultimate needs.

Once the pupil managed to convince himself that vertigo really was not for the birds, his aerial floatation abilities swiftly progressed, along with numerous enjoyable social moments spent with his instructor after hours. Via this, Dick was only five days into his training course when he came clean over what he was desperately seeking, which frustratingly failed to inspire so much as a hint of interest from Jack Elliot.

In fact, it was only a chance remark over a drink the following evening which suddenly inspired his instructor's enthusiasm.

"What, Dick, you are intending to use Handley Page Hastings aircraft for the drop? I was certain that the Nigerian Air Force would utilise their recent Russian

THIRTEEN

aeronautical acquisitions and you would be stuck with Ilyushins, in which I refuse to fly on principle. I am sure that you won't think I look old enough, but as a squaddie, I took part in the last major RAF para operation during the Suez crisis in 1956 and we jumped out of Handley Page Hastings planes. Let me take a proper shufti at your Hollywood film script."

The scene was virtually set and, whilst Richard's qualifying was being celebrated by the two of them – plus some buddies in Guildford's Angel Hotel – on Saturday night, a form of assent was forged.

"Look, Dick, partly because I believe that you still need some nursing in the air, I am on for your foolhardy mission. Nevertheless, because it is a pretty risky undertaking, I shall only accept a squad of volunteers, which may take a few days. All things being equal, however, I should be able to join you in Nigeria within ten days, max. And don't worry over my not obtaining permission because, as usual, I shall accept no interference from my superiors whatsoever."

This result was obviously a great relief, which was considerably enhanced by the fact that Falcon clearly regarded Major Blake's recruiting success as an affront to his tactical views.

Nonetheless, on euphorically sharing his good news with Bill and Toby, Richard did experience a sneaking suspicion that a degree of scepticism still lurked in their congratulations.

This impression inspired him to immediately request Colonel McMillan to increase the number of Force A soldiers in training to four hundred on the basis that there would hopefully be room for most of them in the Cargomasters.

During their coded email exchange, Colin expressed his delight over the imminent arrival of Major Jack Elliot's contingent and readily agreed to include the additional men in his training programme.

He also advised that the paratroops would now be based in Kaduna rather than Zaria and that Captain Leon Balogun was already honing the limited skills of seventy Nigerian parachutists at a more appropriately equipped barracks there. Out of these, fifty would be selected to fly into action with the Parachute Regiment experts, who would also be fine-tuning the Nigerians' abilities on their arrival from the UK.

Paradoxically, changing the parachutist's location proved to be a cardinal saving grace for the entire operation as, in spite of the intense governmental purges, some military locations were still being spied upon, and Zaria was one of them!

In addition, following an observation made by Colin during a short spell spent with him in Zaria on his return to Nigeria, Richard's arduous duties in Kaduna were to become considerably more bearable than he had anticipated.

"Guess who I bumped into the other day in your new location, Dick? Your old pal, Patty Mullion, over whom you almost got posted to mosquito-infested Lafia all those years ago. Her hubby, the colonel, is no more, but she is looking great, bursting with energy and dying to see you

THIRTEEN

again, which I took the liberty of telling her will shortly be possible. As we have considerable delays, due to problems with the Cargomaster renovations, in order to stimulate your leadership qualities, why not get stuck in and enjoy your favourite sport?"

Blake's original meeting with this voluptuous blonde tennis athlete, who was seven years his senior, was in Kaduna at the annual North versus South Nigeria rugby match in 1959.

Although she was ever a firm favourite with the boys, Richard got her attention first at the post-game party when, whilst playing at number eight for the North, he sustained a fractured wrist and was obliged to come off the field early.

A romantic situation then developed when, following a particularly wild party to celebrate a Northern victory, their affinity was consummated on the back seat of her husband's Simca Beaulieu.

However, because of the much-gossiped-about affair that followed, Blake was fortunate to have avoided being cashiered for his sins.

This was due to the fact that Patty's ageing banker husband had been a colonel in the Indian Army and via the 'once an officer, always an officer' tradition, Richard was in effect screwing another officer's wife, an act which was strictly taboo in the British Army.

Fortunately, his new young commanding officer commuted this daunting penalty to a remote posting, which his wayward favourite indefinitely delayed and managed to eventually avoid when he joined the Royal Fusiliers in London.

Now eager to rekindle his former elicit romantic attachment, Richard took Colin's advice and used the phone number he had been given to propose a dinner at the Kaduna club. Patty sounded exactly the same as he remembered her and accepted the invitation with alacrity.

Then, with coquettish waywardness, the ever-outrageous lady provided ideal support for Richard during the intense training programmes in which he was involved during the following three weeks or so.

Also, his sensual and humorous spells in Patty's company helped to divert the guilt that most leaders experience when it becomes their duty to risk the lives of their eager subordinates by exposing them to extreme danger.

Anyway, having ensured that Jack Elliot's experts and Captain Balogun's local force had blended in well, and with all the aircraft now fully operational, within thirty days, Blake and McMillan deemed that their mission was at last ready for a green light.

FOURTEEN

Although Shen Wing's judgement could occasionally become distorted by his impetuous and vindictive nature, he was fundamentally a highly efficient, guileful soldier whose only dread was military incongruity.

Thus, he was frustratingly nonplussed by the glaring inadequacies of the host that his adversaries were preparing to field against Berundi.

The activities of Wing and Unegby had recently been considerably impaired by Victor Adesola's purge of Nigerian collaborators, which had been extremely thorough, particularly in the former Biafran zone and Lagos. Nonetheless, a fair number of them had managed to slip through the net and a diminished team of informers had been maintained.

Currently, by far the most important of these was Corporal Ahmed Musa who, having just been stationed as a Zaria replacement, was able to report back on what was occurring at the new government special operations base there.

It was Colonel McMillan's activities here that were perplexing Colonel Wing as it appeared that only four hundred or so soldiers were being trained to attack an objective where they could to be confronted by a force of over four times that number. This meant that, even if McMillan was confident that his contingent would gain the element of total surprise over partially trained soldiers, his approach was still grossly over-optimistic from a tactical point of view.

This incongruous numerical situation was verified by the fact that there were only two aircraft on standby at Zaria's aerodrome for air-lifting the attacking force and their motor transports.

To cap it all, Blake, who was McMillan's only back-up man that possessed any personal knowledge of the target's configuration, had disappeared and was generally supposed to have returned to the UK.

Shen's confusion was largely due to his firm belief that the informers still in place were loyal and this misconception deprived him of one vital piece of intelligence. To his eventual detriment, the colonel was unaware that he had been betrayed in Kaduna by Sergeant Kelechi Lanacho, who, in order to avoid sharing martyrdom with many of his former co-conspirators, had become a government double agent.

Unfortunately, though, because of an isolation strategy recently imposed by the rebels, Lanacho was unaware of Corporal Musa's traitorous activities in Zaria so was

FOURTEEN

unable to warn McMillan that any chance of a Force A's attack being a surprise had been blown.

Nevertheless, the sergeant's new patriotic cooperation had maintained the secrecy of Blake's air corps training programmes at the Kaduna base.

However, in spite of his sense of foreboding, the ever-vigilant Chinese colonel meticulously developed a solid Berundi defence strategy where, even if his troops were a mixed bag, he made full use of his abundant weaponry availability.

Thus, physical defence measures against what was bound to be a night attack would be situated along to the semi-completed low wall which surrounded the complex at a distance of two hundred yards.

For this, heavily protected arc lights were set up and Belgian medium machine guns installed at seventy-yard intervals, which would be primarily manned by the Chinese instructors.

From a personnel point of view, Colonel Wing decided that fifteen hundred soldiers were sufficiently trained for combat, who would be deployed along the fortifications, armed with Lee-Enfield and FN self-loading rifles, twenty 303 light machine guns, plus hand grenades.

In addition, the remainder of his fifty oriental specialists would be patrolling the base's approach road.

What could possibly go wrong?

***

McMillan and Blake's code word 'Barnacles' triggered

a pre-arranged schedule which was geared to an arrival of their aircraft at Quala between 12.30am and 1am, for which full permission had duly been granted by the Central African Republic.

As anticipated, landing on such a primitive airfield proved to be a testing exercise for the Cargomasters, with much bumping through the flattish bush land adjacent to and at each end of the airstrips.

Notwithstanding these initial tribulations, however, by 1.45am, the troops, plus their personnel carriers, had been disembarked and the Handley Page Hastings para planes were lined up and ready to go.

Richard put his arm around his old friend's shoulders. "Well, Colin, after much farting about, I believe that it is at last time to get our show on the road. Don't forget that once you have anaesthetised any CAR guards you encounter on crossing the border, you are only a couple of miles from the base, so advancing much further should be on foot, as per our much-maligned plan. As you have about an hours' drive until then, I will hope to hear that you are in position by around 0330 hours. Take good care, buddy, and good luck."

After a brief embrace, Colin responded, "Same to you, Dick, and you seem to have been blessed by a fullish moon in addition to the camp's lights to help guide you in. We have to get this one right, if only to prove everyone else wrong, especially your shit of a spy boss."

Shen Wing's first defence strategy blunder turned out to be his posting of patrols on the base's approach road, as their presence gave a premature warning to his enemies that their arrival had been anticipated.

FOURTEEN

Much to Richard's amazement, it was only 3.05am when he received Colin's trigger code word 'Parapluie'. However, the cause for signal being made prematurely became apparent when, on flying in for the drop, it was clear that Force A was being heavily engaged with concentrated fire from just outside the compound.

Blake turned to Jack Elliot at his elbow. "Fucking hell, we've been rumbled. I wonder what surprises the bastards have lined up for us?"

"Well, my friend, let's get down there and find out for ourselves," was the stalwart reply.

Unbelievably, though, whilst Richard was gearing up to perform his gut-wrenching jump, the lack of any retaliation from below suggested that their bellicose hosts had not anticipated an aerial visitation. In fact, it was only during the Hastings's second run-in, which was necessitated by the confined landing zone, that a few machine guns erratically attempted anti-aircraft fire.

As Elliot was about to guide his former student into space, he remarked, "Let's hope that the death and destruction that we are about to inflict on the barracks will take some heat off Colin. It certainly appears that he is in desperate need of some back-up."

Amazingly, most of the paratroop force managed to land more or less on target. Then, within fifteen minutes, their massed fire power in the form of incendiary missiles and anti-tank rockets reduced the military complex to flaming, crumbling ruins, out of which numerous screaming smouldering beings fled in terror.

Disastrously, though, before this occurred, McMillan's Force A, having successfully driven off the initial welcoming party, were suddenly illuminated and raked by lethal machine-gun fire, the intensity of which obliged them to go to ground.

Nevertheless, all was not yet lost as Shen Wing's shock and fury over the unforeseen airborne invasion had plunged him into an atypical mode of indecision.

For a few critical minutes he was in a dilemma as to whether he should deploy a detachment to deal with the para invaders before or after advancing his men to finish off the battered enemy force before him.

By the time he decided upon the latter course, the destruction of the main compound was becoming dramatically apparent, and to make matters worse, injured novice recruits were fleeing from their bombarded barrack blocks into his ranks.

The nett result was a commanding officer's biggest nightmare, when a majority of his subordinates lose their moral fibre and become incapable of functioning.

With such a situation now proliferating, when the colonel eventually gave the order to advance, no one moved and, in spite of aggressive encouragement from their instructors, the stunned soldiers' rate of fire steadily diminished.

Then, after Shen shot a senior recruit who had thrown down his rifle, serenaded by the roaring crackle of their burning accommodation, his semi-trained army disintegrated as a majority of the men disappeared into the bush.

FOURTEEN

Meanwhile Richard Blake, Jack Elliot and the paratroops were amazed when they encountered zero resistance as they advanced to aid what was left of Force A.

Their heavy casualties included McMillan who, having taken a bullet in the thigh, was unkindly ribbed by Major Elliot. "Well done, you lucky bastard, at least you have experienced some action and excitement tonight. I have never been so bored in my life. Honestly, I go through the paraphernalia of giving your mate the balls to use a parachute and all I get for thanks is taking part in a demolition exercise. I am certain that my valiant volunteers here will never forgive me for involving them in such a dreary venture!"

Richard's comment at this point was, "Ignore this sadistic bastard, Colin, and I am so sorry that your lot suffered more than a few fatalities. At least that scratch will qualify you and the other wounded for a spell in the Berundi hooker's training college where you will be taken care of in their castration hospital."

"Trust you to know about that, Dick, but go easy on the humour, both of you, as this bloody well hurts. At least you can now settle the score for Tony's foul slaughter with that mildewed piece of shit over there."

The confused, humiliated and embittered Shen Wing was shackled to a nearby gun carriage in the heavy weaponry storage area of the complex, so Richard casually wandered over to him and delivered a resounding kick in the testicles, which welled up tears in his vicious little bloodshot eyes.

On strolling back to McMillan, who was about to be carted off on a stretcher, he remarked, "There, I have done my bit and decided that the little swine's limited future would be more appropriately catered for by your ingenuity, combined with some traditional Nigerian cures for demonic misconduct. I shall pop in later to check that you are being properly attended to by a sympathetic nurse!"

A more satisfying final encounter for Blake was with Unegby, whom he visited at noon in a cellar beneath his former office.

"Albert, great to see you again, and my friends and I are proud and delighted to have relieved you of your presidential burden. You are also being deprived of your responsibility for disciplining, training and selling your fellow human beings, who I am sure will all remember you with affection for your selfless dedication to their well-being in the past. In fact, as my old girlfriend Nadia was craving so much to visit you, I gave her permission to pop down here earlier this morning, without realising that you are clearly into masochistic bondage. She must have been feeling extra passionate as she seems to have marred your immaculate image by permitting blood from your mouth and nose to discolour your hard-won medals. In addition to which, she has allowed more blood to stain the flies and trouser legs of your uniform and then forgotten to untie you. I must ensure that she comes back and apologises."

The poltroon instantly burst into tears. "I implore you to not let that woman anywhere near me again. She

FOURTEEN

tried to slice by balls off with a bread knife and it was only the guard who prevented her in case I bled to death and cheated the hangman, as he put it."

"For God's sake stop snivelling, Mr Ex-President. I am surprised that Nadia could find your balls in the first place, but she was probably just giving you some advance practice for enduring what the traditional Nigerian penalty for treason might be.

Even though you were an accessory to my dear friend's murder, as a true Brit I would have settled for your expiry at the end of a rope but, sadly for both of us, I shall not be orchestrating your death. Farewell. You will not be seeing much of anybody very soon!"

Following a latish booze-up with Jack and other main players at Colin's hospital bedside to celebrate 'mission accomplished', Richard hijacked the Berundi Liar Jet next day for the first stage of his flight back to the UK via Kaduna.

Whilst collecting his belongings there, he received a Falcon signal insisting that his very first priority when he arrived in London had to be reporting to him. Twenty hours later, Blake was in his bête noire's MI6 office at noon.

Amazingly, the colonel appeared to be in good humour for once and actually smiled and shook hands on greeting him.

"Now then, Jingles, before you exercise your right to gloat, I offer you my heartiest congratulations for achieving the totally illogical. Because you are an extremely difficult man to hate, I found myself uncharacteristically concerned over the probability of your permanent departure. Also, as I am obviously getting soft, I recently took the liberty of accessing your London home in order to house a visiting foreign agent. Her code name is 'Pearl' and she is irrationally most eager to see you."

As Dick was to discover, the old bastard had actually got something right for a change!

This book is printed on paper from sustainable sources managed under the Forest Stewardship Council (FSC) scheme.

It has been printed in the UK to reduce transportation miles and their impact upon the environment.

For every new title that Matador publishes, we plant a tree to offset CO_2, partnering with the More Trees scheme.

For more about how Matador offsets its environmental impact, see www.troubador.co.uk/about/